TEN PLANETS

ALSO BY YURI HERRERA

A Silent Fury: The El Bordo Mine Fire
The Transmigration of Bodies
Signs Preceding the End of the World
Kingdom Cons

TEN PLANETS

Stories

YURI HERRERA

Translated from the Spanish by Lisa Dillman

Graywolf Press

"The Science of Extinction" appeared in the *Iron Lattice*. "The Obituarist" appeared in *Washington Square Review*. "House Taken Over" appeared in *Words Without Borders*. "The Objects" [#1] appeared in *Epoch*. "The Objects" [#2] appeared in *World Literature Today*. "Flat Map" and "Obverse" appeared in *Zyzzyva*. "The Monsters' Art" appeared in *Southwest Review*. "Appendix 15, Number 2: The Exploration of Agent Probii" appeared in *Boston Review*. "The Last Ones" appeared in *Conjunctions*.

This publication is made possible, in part, by the voters of Minnesota through a Minnesota State Arts Board Operating Support grant, thanks to a legislative appropriation from the arts and cultural heritage fund. Significant support has also been provided by the McKnight Foundation, the Lannan Foundation, the Amazon Literary Partnership, and other generous contributions from foundations, corporations, and individuals. To these organizations and individuals we offer our heartfelt thanks.

MINNESOTA
STATE ARTS BOARD

CLEAN
WATER
LAND &
LEGACY
AMENDMENT

Published by Graywolf Press
212 Third Avenue North, Suite 485
Minneapolis, Minnesota 55401

All rights reserved.

www.graywolfpress.org

Published in the United States of America

ISBN 978-1-64445-223-3 (paperback)
ISBN 978-1-64445-224-0 (ebook)

2 4 6 8 9 7 5 3 1
First Graywolf Printing, 2023

Library of Congress Control Number: 2022938630

Cover design: Carlos Esparza

Cover photo: Levi Stute

CONTENTS

The Science of Extinction   3

Whole Entero   5

The Obituarist   9

The Cosmonaut   15

House Taken Over   25

Consolidation of Spirits   31

The Objects   35

The Objects   41

Flat Map   45

The Earthling   47

The Monsters' Art   53

Obverse   57

Inventory of Human Diversity   59

Zorg, Author of the *Quixote*   63

The Other Theory   71

The Conspirators   73

Appendix 15, Number 2: The Exploration of Agent Probii   85

Living Muscle   89

The Last Ones   91

Warning   99

Translator's Note   103

TEN PLANETS

THE SCIENCE OF EXTINCTION

When the man realized he'd soon be lost, he took out a small yellow card, wrote four words, and placed it on the sill of the window he looked out every day upon waking.

He no longer remembered the names of the people he'd once lived with. A wife, a daughter, a son, someone else. Cuddles, squabbles, drinks, doors, greetings. Then slices of greetings, doors, drinks, squabbles, cuddles. Slices ever thinner. At first he'd tried to boost his concentration by counting from a hundred to zero several times a day, but now he had started losing his way around seventy, and all the numbers began to resemble whimsical versions of zero.

He no longer recalled his date of birth. Or the city where he was born. Or his parents. Had he had parents? There was no one left to tell him this either.

He knew that things were going on inside his body, that he needed medication, but he would happen upon it only by accident, walking into the kitchen and seeing a bag of rice, or lying down and discovering the pills by his bed. For he'd also forgotten what to call that chill in his stomach, that defeat in his bones.

There were moments of wordless euphoria, when he'd marvel at his lack of fear of a noise or an object he could no longer name. And he decided—and could recall this decision though not the exact words with which he'd made it—that he was no longer going to lament. Perhaps it wasn't a decision but a strategy for survival or a new aptitude.

Sometimes he would see something, an object with four legs and a flat surface, and call it *cup*. And he saw that this was good. Sometimes he noticed something fluttering in the wind and it didn't occur to him to call it anything in any lasting way, but he saw that this too was good.

The increasingly depopulated world rewilding on the other side of the window was full of other things he couldn't recall having paid attention to. Horizons, dust, corners. And the silences.

The too-many silences.

The reason he didn't get lost was because of the silences. At times he yearned to walk and walk with no destination, but the silences, each so distinct, came one after another: an impenetrable jungle of silences overwhelmed him, and then he'd go back inside.

One day a disturbance appeared before him: an undulation of swirling sounds, colors, velocities. He was transfixed for quite some time (which might have been a second).

Then he decided to address it. In a stammer of random syllables that in his head formed a crystal clear sentence, he said:

"I found a message that someone left us on a card. It says, 'Everyone is going away.'"

He waited a brief eternity for the reply, then the little swirl spun again and vanished.

WHOLE ENTERO

The vespertine coliform existed, complexly, in the summer of 1999, in the region of Norfolk, England; specifically, in the town of Sheringham; to be still more exact, in the small intestine of one Roger Wolfeston, former manufacturer of fake documents, who'd had a bit of a boon. This blunder of nature resulted from the unexpectedly swift evolution of a bacterium of the entero-bacterial order—a *Citrobacter,* since we've unloosed the illusion of precision—entering into contact with a lysergic acid in the microvilli of Wolfeston's large intestine. The improbable chemical reaction triggered by the prolonged exposure of the saprophytic flora to the acid—which Mr. Wolfeston had picked up on his last trip to London and which did not yield the expected outcome— led the aforementioned bacteria to undergo unforeseen changes in the adolescence of its existence, though none that made it lethal or diminished its fermentative qualities. It's just that the bacteria, miraculously, gained consciousness.

The vespertine coliform made a leap from eternal wintering to the perception of the immeasurable: a wordless splendor. The vertigo of fluids, vestiges of earlier ebullience, angles and surfaces of other bacteria, all of it pointed to her place as the center of the universe; she was the crossroads through which meaning

was given to what we approximate with names like *temperature,*
light, and *time.*

The universe's distinction led her to name it by gradations
of consciousness: the great intensity with which she perceived a
crest or the emptiness of certain times of day became the thing's
name. She learned first to wait, then to yearn, and finally to
imagine. And with the realization that what *was* was not what
was but what could be, she began to erect for herself a place in
the world. The understanding that ensued from that moment is
what has come to be called *the placid eve of the coliform*: the period
in which she made unbridled plans to bust out of her field of mo-
tility, traverse uncharted zones of the intestine, and leave a trace
of her scourge at every point.

The vespertine coliform managed to sophisticate her emotions to such a degree that, prior to the Apocalypse, she succeeded in knowing existential anguish. She surrendered herself
to the feeling of having lost something she'd never had, on discovering that the garden that housed her was beginning, inex-
orably, to decay. Why? Why must everything come to an end?
Why had it begun to begin with? It would have done no good
for anyone to inform her that there was a primary host and that
he, Roger Wolfeston, broker of false papers, was dying of absti-
nence in the rehabilitation center to which he'd been sentenced
by the law; no good even if it were communicable, for the scale
of those events was so inconceivable (the existence of an organ-
ism so enormous and labyrinthine that it could host millions like
her!) that the only way of relating it to her reality was by means
of a fiction. For a moment she intuited this solution—religion—
but by that point ennui and loneliness had descended.

She, the vespertine coliform, was one light of awareness among
billions, the vastest population on an earth she had never managed to conceive, but the feeling of emptiness so overwhelmed her

that, on glimpsing the divine solution, she discarded it instantly, convinced that if she could articulate something so immense, if there existed an instrument—words—with which to formulate it, then that thing was impossible; no, the grandiose and definitive could never be defined by the brief and simple and elementary. And long before Roger Wolfeston could relieve himself with a needle, relapse, and die, the vespertine coliform fell ill from sadness and, almost without realizing, was extinguished forever.

THE OBITUARIST

On the way to the scene of death, the obituarist groused about fucking invisibility: Fucking invisibility; as if I didn't know that this empty street, just like every empty street in every other city, is teeming with people.

The only ones who could be seen were the ones whose jobs required public visibility: delivery people, plumbers, painters, etceteras. They got badges, and when they put them on, became what they had to be and only what they had to be: delivery person, plumber, painter, etcetera, each covered by a neon silhouette. The rest wandered about unseen, protected by a buffer that blocked images, sounds, odors, keeping their bodies at a distance. Which meant that, walking down a deserted street, you'd bump into soft lumps that knocked you gently from side to side. Only in the heaviest congestion could people's contours be seen and thus avoided, but there was never any need to see faces or expressions, feel bones or fat. Ever. The buffer served as a laissez-passer, allowing travel, and owners could take them off only indoors.

Yeah, big deal, the obituarist muttered, as he did each day: He could still sense them at that very moment. Their irritated presence, their contained rage. He might be able to stop seeing others but he couldn't stop sensing their essence. Sooner or later even children learn that hiding your eyes doesn't actually make things disappear. I can sense them right *now*, he repeated, making his way through the subdued reproach of those standing aside to let him pass.

He reached the building, saw the elevator doors open, and tried to get on but bounced gently off the people inside. He walked up three flights. There were already two badges at the scene of death. Certifiers. They certified the dead's death, and he recounted the living's life. Though the government possessed every piece of electronic communication anyone had ever sent in their life, the obituarist didn't use them to tell their story, basing it instead on what the living had left behind. His obituaries were wildly successful. The public devoured them, not only to learn what a person had done without having had to put up with them while they were alive, but because many had high hopes that accumulating certain things would enable them to manipulate obituarists into telling better stories about them.

"Lotta people out today?" asked one of the badges, neon pulsating with each word.

"Same as ever," replied the obituarist. "But the most important person in the room ain't complaining."

The obituarist didn't like people criticizing his work. He prided himself on being punctual. Though it might seem his profession was the one least requiring haste, he knew how important it was to get to a story before its parts began to dissolve.

The certifier who'd spoken pulsed softly in silence. The other said:

"Nothing new. Guy had a functioning heart one second and a nonfunctioning heart a second later."

The second certifier was, most likely, a woman.

He observed the body. It looked tired, even in death. The kind of tiredness that was no longer common: hands wrinkled, skin weathered, a rictus of severe resignation. While he studied the body, the certifiers put away their instruments and were already on their way out when the obituarist said:

"Don't go."

He thought he felt *something*.

"Is there someone else I need to see?" he asked.

The certifiers pulsed doubtfully, containing more than emitting their neon. They didn't understand what he meant.

"Is it just the two of you?" he went on. "No one else came with you?"

"Two, as it should be," said the one who'd spoken first.

"Wait for me at the door."

The certifiers obeyed, no clear emotion discernible from their silhouettes.

He began searching through what the dead man had left behind. Kitchen utensils. Few. Generic. Indicating no interest in complicated dishes. Furniture. An armchair, a table, a chair, a bed, a dresser. Generic. Made to meet basic needs. And clothes. Lots of clothes. Odd. People didn't tend to accumulate clothes now that buffers were mandatory; the obituarist had even found people who no longer bothered to get dressed. And this dead guy had a lot of clothes. But . . . generic. Identical. The obituarist looked at them for a bit—looked at the clothes, then looked at the body. Looked at the clothes, then looked at the body. Kept searching. On the dresser he found documents from the dead man's job, including pictures of the sort of metal balls that had become popular. The obituarist had come upon them in many homes, but not in this one, that of a man who had sold them. He felt curious about this man who'd left him almost nothing to work with: this was a list, not a life. Whatever he'd been inside could hardly be divined by his belongings.

But the belongings didn't go with what he was piecing together from the body. He thought this, and went to observe it again.

Then he began pacing the tiny apartment, one side to the other, over and over. He stopped. Had the certifiers been able to see him under the neon, they'd have noted that for a second it looked like he was trying to hang in the air. He kept walking. Stopped. Continued. Stopped.

Now he was sure.

He turned to the certifiers and said:

"You can go. Close the door on your way out."

The certifiers walked out. He could see, beneath the door, the glow of their neon, pulsing. No doubt they were commenting on the obituarist's behavior.

He took his time going over the furniture, clothes, dresser once more. Without much effort. Almost offhanded. Until again he felt clearly a spot giving off condensed tension, placed the chair in front of it, sat down, took off his badge, and stared at the empty space. After a few seconds he said:

"Who is this man?"

Silence.

The obituarist stood, felt in front of himself for a second, and then pushed the soft blob as hard as he could. Guy'd have no way out of that corner.

That was when the other man took off his buffer. Before the obituarist could make out any details, he got a whiff of the guy's smell, not a dirty smell or a dusty one but the smell of nervous sweat. Then he saw him. He was a soft man, a man who seemed to have been wearing buffers since before they were even invented. He must have been older than the obituarist, but not as old as the man laid out on the floor. There was plenty of hair on his head, and it was neatly combed.

"Who is he?" the obituarist said.

The man leaned back into the corner, glanced down at the man on the floor, and said:

"I don't know, someone I found on the street and invited in."

"What do you mean *someone you found*?"

The man waffled his hands vaguely, searching for a way to explain. Then let them drop.

"I sensed him passing by. I don't know how to explain it . . . I sensed him in his buffer."

The obituarist said nothing.

"I sensed he was dying," the man said.

The obituarist turned back to the dead man. The other guy did the same. They remained thus for some time.

"So, fuck him, right?" the obituarist said finally. "You son of a bitch."

He stood and called the certifiers back. What was the matter, they wanted to know. Theft of history, he told them. They'd be right there.

The man was now crumpled in the corner like a discarded overcoat. The obituarist said nothing. He had nothing to say. But he stared at him.

The certifiers arrived. They pinned on the man a badge identifying him as state property, and led him to the door. Before leaving he turned back to the obituarist.

"Tell me, what were you going to say about me?"

The obituarist didn't so much as glance at him. He gestured at the man on the floor to the certifiers.

"Have someone come for him," he said. "And let me know when you find his address."

The certifiers pulsed in assent and led the thief out.

The obituarist sat back down in the chair and remained there a few more minutes. He wondered if he too were not a stand-in for a dead man. Was that how they saw him as he walked around, all lit up, among the invisible? Like someone who keeps looking when there's nothing more to see? Perhaps that was why they consumed his obituaries, to discover whether it was possible to have a hand in the lie.

He tutted, suspicious of himself.

Turning on his badge, he closed the door, descended the three flights of stairs, and walked out into the empty street.

THE COSMONAUT

I've found unimaginable treasures, solved age-old enigmas, encountered darker-than-dark spirits, all by nose. Not mine: the noses of others. I still recall my first victory, the day I demonstrated the scientificity of my hermeneutics, when I realized the nose is a map. In the beginning, like any dimwit, I thought every nose was an approximation of the same place: a more or less precipitous mountain, with caverns on one of its slopes through which air flowed. Until I realized that the nose needs interpretation: its curvature, its scars, its spots, pores, and hairs, the narrowness of its nasal cavities as well as its relationship to the rest of the mug. A nose is a map, though not one that resembles the actual territory it delineates. This should be obvious on any given map, yet we tend to believe that the representation of an object must be similar to the object. Absurd. Each nose describes a place, but you've got to know how it speaks of that place (yes, noses *speak*), and above all you've got to deduce, with no obvious clues, where the devil that place is—where, of all places in existence.

It was one of those uncanny things, like when you're thinking of someone and suddenly see them turn the corner. An old girlfriend of mine, one who had enough sense to get away from me for her own good, had a tiny little nose, double-snubbed at the tip: dainty and deformed at the same time. On the day in question, I stared and stared at it and she sat there looking troubled and troubled, because though I'd explained what I was observing, she was unconvinced by my speculations:

"Each nose," I said, pointing out various aspects of hers, "is the code to a secret, because with every inhalation, tiny particles of the landscape are introduced into the body, because the landscape is constantly decomposing: chairs, concrete, people, everything disintegrates like a dandelion in the breeze. When you inhale, those tiny particles not only begin creating—inside you—the code to unlock something unique in the world, they also shape your nose, give it the subtle attributes of that thing, but it has to be recognized. And therein lies the problem."

And this speaking-while-staring became a stroke of insight. All at once I saw the way to read a nose—its grammar—as well as the secret that *this particular nose* was revealing.

Ana, which was the name of the girl in question, had said at the start of our romance that her parents had never been willing to provide any details about a twin brother whom she had once had and then no longer had, because he died when Ana was still very young. Her parents would neither confirm nor deny, just let her suspicions grow. But on seeing her that day, on seeing the map that was her nose, shaped by the dust of her childhood, together with the patina of her rooms and the evaporated sweat of her parents each time she asked them about him, I knew how to read it, as sure as if it were the only way to reveal the exact location of his hiding place. I turned and, under the watchful eyes of her parents, who were growing bored of spying on us, crossed the living room without turning to look at them, went into Ana's room, moved aside the small bed Ana had slept in since she was a child, pulled up a floorboard, and there, beneath it, in a shoebox, lay the tiny skeleton, dressed in a blue crocheted baby jacket, just as Ana's nose had told me: perfect in appearance, like the home, split in two—the evil fragility of it all.

Ana left me shortly thereafter, perhaps because she couldn't stand to be with the one who'd revealed something the inhabitants of the house knew but had chosen not to discuss, or perhaps because of the inappropriately triumphal cry I let out upon discovering the box and opening it, so unlike her horrified whimper; or maybe the whole affair made her wonder what kind of person she herself was, to be in a relationship with a person like me.

So, as I've said, each nasal map is made up of the shards of that which it conceals—the shards of that which it reveals; it's not merely an exalted figment of the imagination but concrete evidence. The problem is that the thing being sought is not always openly admitted to; sometimes the person bearing the map hasn't even admitted it to themselves. They seek and seek, yet do not seek. Each nose is a code, and yet it's nearly impossible to know to what. You can take anyone, *anyone*, and study their environs, nose around inside them, as it were, listen to their fears, intuit their weaknesses, and then deduce what secret keys they've been inhaling, the way they've been led in a certain direction, albeit unawares. A lover's perfume, the scrape of their shoes, the stench of their desire for another person, the spleen that ruptured after all hell broke loose, the compactness of being locked in a trunk, the landscape as it changes on the way to hide the trunk, the damp rock under which it was abandoned. No matter how far the thing gets, or how far they get from the thing, the nose gets hooked and holds on to its traces like a coordinate.

Once I'd perfected my technique, I exploited it. In the beginning, prospective clients wrote me off because my skill struck them as a con or they plainly took me for a pervert (and in this they were not mistaken). But since someone granted me the benefit of the doubt and I proved my efficacy, fame ensued. If you haven't heard of me, it's because this is a wretched age in which all is soon forgotten, as if each time anyone turned their head, they were awakening from amnesia.

I unearthed mislaid documents, jewels too well hidden, a couple of dogs, a stole made from an extinct animal, seventy-eight keys, loaned-out books, socks, even a small country that cartographers had been unable to keep pace with. It was all a matter of reading the nose while asking a few questions to figure out how to connect what I'd read to the extra-nosarial world. Is that blemish a voyage? This deformed septum—is it a tragedy or merely a souvenir from some drunken brawl? What emotional chasm is described by a dorsum so slender over nostrils so flared? Where did the person spend their childhood? When they awoke beside their lover, what was the first thing they noticed?

Still, my most interesting cases were not the ones where I actually had to recover exactly what I was told to recover but the ones where I was called in for one thing and realized that the person in possession of the nose actually sought another, or, better still, that in no way did they want me to find the thing I'd been hired to find. I would turn up and start studying the map on someone's face. And discover a series of signs that were mutually compatible but did not resolve the matter I'd been hired to address. Sometimes because there was someone else in the room, other times because the person didn't know whether they wanted the matter to be resolved.

All of this to explain what happened with the cosmonaut.

One day two men came to my door, dressed so as to look inconspicuous yet still threatening: one in a blue suit, the other in a blue suit, both wearing gray ties. But though the nose of the first seemed to point to the location of a runaway wife, that of the second was clearly the blueprint needed to unearth a photo album. They might have said Good afternoon and even Please, but more than that there was an urgency and determination to their gestures that made it clear they knew exactly what they wanted of me, and it wasn't in me to deny them. Even so, I asked:

"Do you know my rate?"

One of them, the one in blue, said, "Raise a hand," and the other, the one in blue, added:

"Point to anything at all and it's yours."

They said nothing on the way. From the back seat, though, I was able to discern from the profile of one of them—the one in blue—that he was keeping a secret involving the other, and that the other didn't know.

The cosmonaut was an imposing and terrified man. They had him in an aseptic dungeon that plenty of people would have paid millions for. No natural light, but lots of open space. It was like a barn that had been done up in multiple shades of white. In the center was a well-made bed and a table with two chairs facing each other. And at the time I didn't know the man was a cosmonaut.

How could I, given that he was in a cosmonaut suit—who sits at a table like that? Because he was sitting at a Formica table. A bottle of water and a glass before him, his helmet resting on his legs. The cosmonaut had not drunk.

I turned to glance at the two men, awaiting instructions. One of them, the one in blue, didn't say a word, and the other didn't make a gesture. I gathered that they wanted to see what I could learn without being given any information. I sat down across from the cosmonaut and gave a slight nod, the merest hint of a nod. The cosmonaut pupiled his eyes almost imperceptibly in acknowledgment of my deference.

He was gripped by fear, but it was still him doing the gripping and not the other way around. He let it show with the equanimity of someone who had enough self-respect not to hide behind a mask of pride, which inspired my respect.

The cosmonaut was black. His nose was at once elegant and granitic, as though sculpted in a rapture of magnificence. His nostrils flared only slightly, though it looked as if they might activate forcefully at any moment. His skin was smooth and taut, save for a few incongruously open pores, less wide than they were deep. And there was something else, a small mole whose hue I was unable to decipher, gray or translucent, abstrusing itself on the upper cusp of the bridge, as if about to dive into his left eye.

This map was different from anything I'd ever seen, pointing to something whose magnitude I could glimpse, though I couldn't see its substance.

I got up from my chair and circled the cosmonaut, eyeing him the whole time. I positioned myself beside him and, crouching down, from there observed the contours of his face. How to understand it? Then the cosmonaut moved his head in a way that, from my perspective, made the faint bluish light of the room slowly appear, as if day were dawning behind his head, and I understood.

I asked the men to step out of the room with me. Once outside, I said:

"What exactly are you looking for?"

They consulted each other in silence, not moving a muscle, not even looking at each other. Then the one in blue said:

"Have you finished your examination?"

"Give me another minute. Wait here."

They consulted in silence once more and the one in blue nodded.

I returned to the room and again sat down facing the cosmonaut. I had seen the internal logic of the map, the way it triangulated and pointed, but not its points of reference. (A map, however eloquent it may be, is useless if there is nothing familiar that casts it toward one's coordinates.) I could sense that he wouldn't give me the answer, because that would have been giving it to the men who'd imprisoned him. But *I* needed to know.

"Keep whatever you need to keep to yourself, keep me in the dark, but tell me how you found what you found."

The cosmonaut blinked, his lashes long like windshield wipers, as though sweeping away the light before his eyes.

"No cosmonaut has come closer to a comet than I have. I traveled two years to find it. They sent me on my own, to keep costs down: they had little hope I'd be able to get as close as I did, which was useful for them to see if I could endure not just solitude but long-distance solitude. Ha! All that technology to measure solitude. By the end of those two years I was not only close enough to take samples but—*this is the important part*—to *touch* its wake, though from that distance it didn't look like a wake but a river whose water had split into drops a great distance apart. Then they said okay, all over, time for me to turn back. But I wasn't ready. I hadn't traveled all the way to a place where my home was but a twinkle, only to turn around without *knowing* what it was I'd seen. And I decided to venture out."

"A very particular spacewalk, no doubt," I cut in, "but not exactly anything new."

"No," he said, quietly but with such force and clarity it was as if a stone had emerged from his mouth, "no, *but I took off my helmet.*"

He said this and grasped the helmet on his legs through the visor hole. I looked at him, holding my breath as if it were me, in that moment, who was out in space.

"For how long?"

"Really? That's what you want to know? I'm here, aren't I? Do you still not see what I'm talking about?"

I held his gaze, ashamed, and nodded.

"Anyway," he said. "Ten seconds. That's what the alarm said. But to me it was an infinite period of learning. No, not learning—impregnation. The learning came later . . . I don't know if I can tell you what I learned, what I know . . ." He stared at his hands for a moment and then looked straight at me once more, as though fascinated by what he knew, rather than afraid of what he knew. "What I do know is that I saw more than I was supposed to see. You do understand what I mean by *see*, right?"

I heard both the guy in blue and the other one, the one in blue, restlessing on the other side of the door. Our minute was up.

"But there must be something you can tell me."

"You won't understand it, they won't either, but I'm telling you: I felt this energetic cold, not merely a lack of warmth but a fast-moving cold, almost alive, as my blood and skin grew hot. Then I sensed the comet. Not what the instruments had captured but the *experience* of the comet. Where it came from. Or, more like, how *other places* had witnessed *it*."

And I saw something, not in his nose but in his voice, saw it, though this was not my specialty: the intention behind what he was saying, the reason he couldn't reveal what he'd understood. It wasn't that he amassed secrets, like me; it was that this one was about a place that, if he revealed it, they would want to go.

I got up without a word and walked out into the hallway. One of the men, the one in blue, had cocked a gun inside a jacket pocket.

"Man's fried," I said. "There's nothing there. Just his brain, which is still baking away."

"So why does it seem like he's holding out on something? Why isn't he raving aloud?"

"It's a religious thing. I'm sure you've seen this type of stuff before."

It was banal, but I had faith in the banality of the powerful.

"How banal," the one in blue remarked. He opened the door, looked in at the cosmonaut, clucked his tongue in disdain, turned without closing the door, and disappeared with the one in blue down the hall of the immaculate prison.

I peeked into the room.

"Thank you," I said to the cosmonaut. "And don't think I'm doing it for you. I'm doing it because I know what happens when you find what you're looking for."

And then I too left.

HOUSE TAKEN OVER

&°°° couldn't be happier. @°°° couldn't be happier. The twins, *~ and #~, couldn't be happier. Roanoke, the dog, was less enthusiastic, but agreed to lie in a corner of the laundry room, which hollowed itself out graciously as he circled half a dozen times before finding the ideal position.

When the sun beat down, the windows would darken and the temperature cooled. When the traffic outside was very loud, white noise was deployed to eclipse it. When it rained, the roof seemed to interpret the drops, amplifying or silencing them so they didn't sound threatening.

One day when *~ and #~ were running around the house, *~ tripped over his shoelaces and fell. Before his head could hit the corner of a table and tear his skin or knock him out, the table moved a few inches back and *~ banged his hands hard enough to learn a lesson but not so hard that he hurt himself. From that point on, the children's shoes would sort of suction themselves to the floor if they failed to tie their laces immediately after putting on their shoes. The house was learning.

It absorbed odors, cleaned up spills, adjusted the light to favor anyone looking in the mirror.

One night &°°° awoke to the sound of someone attempting to

open one of the living room windows: she could hear the sash sliding. She shook @°°°'s shoulder and in a very soft voice told him that someone was in the house. They got up. &°°° went to check on the twins, and @°°° went to check on Roanoke. Roanoke usually leapt up and alerted them to the slightest sound at night, so something must have happened to him. But @°°° found him curled up in his corner, the wall bulging over him protectively. Smelling @°°°, Roanoke lifted his nose for a moment and wagged his tail in recognition but showed no sign of wanting to get up. Then &°°° came to tell him that the twins were fine. And they went to peek into the living room.

The intruder had managed to open the window and was thrusting himself through it. @°°° ran silently into the kitchen and tried to grab a knife from the wooden block where they were kept, but it wouldn't budge even an inch, nor would any of the other knives. Terrified, he saw &°°° standing in the living room doorway and the man's body halfway inside the house and said to himself, "The house doesn't know how to determine what's important." Just then he heard a loud crack and watched as three steel tentacles emerged outside the window, from the foundation, and in the blink of an eye reached into the house, seized the intruder, squeezed until his bones cracked, and flung him out.

The house knew how to determine what was important.

They began to grasp the implications of the house's ability to learn on the day *~ jammed a pencil into one of #~'s legs. &°°° was quick to treat the wound, and @°°° took off his belt to give *~ an educational lash, just one, so *~ would remember that what he'd done was wrong, but as he took a step toward the offending twin, the floor tiles moved and @°°° fell to the ground. Not realizing what had happened, he stood back up, and again the tiles brought him down. &°°° tried to approach from the other side but the moving floor blocked her as well. Roanoke, on the other hand, walked calmly between them, sat down beside *~, licked his face, and lay down unfussed.

The next thing transpired when @°°° saw a fly gadding around his head. He tried to shoo it away but the fly buzzed all the more aggressively around him. @°°° stood up and spread his arms to clap it between his palms, but the moment he began the inward sweep, he heard the crash of crystal shattering behind him. He walked to the kitchen and saw that all the glasses had crashed to the floor, as though they'd been pushed from *inside* the cupboard.

Next it was the door. &°°° walked in from the street, furious for any or all of the reasons why whatever it was the world was becoming would infuriate someone. All the unbreathable air, all the unbreathable people, the distances, the dead birds, the living cockroaches, the lists she was making of all this on her way home. &°°° slammed the door as she walked in, and the moment she slammed it, the roof tiles rattled as obviously as an obvious rattling of roof tiles might be; but this was no seismicky shudder: the house was quaking with rage. &°°° backed up, calling @°°°, #~, and *~, opened the door, took another step backward, out of the house, and as soon as she'd done so the door closed and the roof stopped rattling. &°°° stood there at the door for a few seconds, then tried to open it, but the door would not give. She banged on it and pushed it as she motherfuckered out loud, no luck. Defeated, she sat down on the ground and looked at her shoes crossed at the ankle, thinking not about them or about the house but about how tired and how tired and how very very tired she was. And after thinking so much about her tiredness, her breathing slowed and her body relaxed and suddenly but with no foofaraw the lock clicked open and &°°° gently walked through the door and closed it behind her.

From then on they began to tiptoe around the house, taking

only baby steps, and if an argument was brewing they kept quiet about it, swallowing their wrath till it passed. Around that time they also began to make detours before coming home, or went out on any old pretext and returned much later, all so as not to be inappropriate.

One day when the four of them were out, by chance they met a beggar. @°°° tossed him a coin and the beggar said, "Thank you, sir, nobody's given me anything today, today of all days," and @°°° said, "What's so special about today?" and the beggar said, "It's my birthday, sir," and @°°° said, "Ah," and the four of them kept walking. But suddenly @°°° stopped and said, "I have an idea." The idea had come to him because he now spent a good part of his day trying to come up with things that might control the house's reactions. He took the entire family to a cake shop, they bought a cake and went back to where the beggar was. "Here, this is for you," @°°° said, handing it to him with a spoon. Then they sang Happy Birthday and began clapping rhythmically, the twins jumping up and down with each clap: "Eat it up, Eat it up." Such a racket did they make that more people gathered around the beggar, and everyone clapped, took photos of him on the ground eating his cake, and then showed them to one another.

They returned home happy and self-satisfied, almost as if they themselves had eaten the cake, and had no trouble opening the door. They walked in, sat down in the living room in silence, happy to have found the way to come and go with no trouble. They looked at the walls, the ceiling, the furniture, and then looked at one another with pride.

At this point Roanoke decided he wanted to go out to pee. He walked to the door, and as #~ got up to open it, the door opened on its own, Roanoke went out, and the door closed on its own. The others were momentarily stunned, then laughed and went to look out the window. Roanoke had finished peeing and was taking advantage of the afternoon, living large: he sniffed a bush, gazed up at the power lines, gnawed on a paw. &°°° said, "I'm going to bring him back in," and turned the doorknob but the doorknob wouldn't budge. @°°° tried it too, even #~ and *~ tried it, but no luck. They went to the back door and couldn't open that, or the windows either.

Outside, Roanoke had flipped belly-up on the grass and was scratching his back in primal glee. So high quality were the windows that Roanoke couldn't hear the cries of desperation of &°°° and @°°° and #~ and *~ as they hurled furniture against the glass.

CONSOLIDATION OF SPIRITS

The heroic bureaucrats in charge of planetary withdrawal, having less and less to do (or more and more clarity about what had to be done), created the Spirit Cadastre Administration when they noticed that lightning, thunderbolts, gutturations, suppurations, screeches, and tremors were spreading wildly through the deserted cities. Although entire countries were by then depopulated, the spirits had not come to find nice little apartments for themselves but to err eternally; now, however, all eternities had been condensed into this precise moment on this done-and-dusted planet. Somehow, a consolidation of spirits had occurred.

One of the heroes of the withdrawal was Mr. Bartleby, a man of sorrows who, just when the world seemed abandoned to its fate, had determined that his intervention was vital.

Bartleby took note of each day's occurrences:

"Ectoplasmic argument at number such-and-such, on such-and-such avenue."

"Satanic shriek duel in this-or-that complex, apartment eight."

"Five-week uninterrupted levitation of furniture in domicile x."

"Errant mother in search of her children complains of vexingly loud *poltergeist* phenomenon appearing on every television in mansion y."

And then he would visit the homes.

But Bartleby was special. The methodology employed by other functionaries witnessing the consolidation of spirits had, as ever, consisted of attempting to deny the phenomenon. The bureaucrats would go and confront each spirit, practically pontificating: they would describe the spirit head to toe, or severed neck to floating extremities, and say things such as "This must not be happening, because it cannot be happening, it is but a mirage produced by the refraction of light and atmospheric changes, all the more so in a time such as this, in which the air has become rarefied with this or that chemical element," and if any spirit roared behind them, they'd turn to it and say, "And this, of course, is a conjunction of vibrations owing to the micro-tremors occurring in the terrestrial cortex at an unparalleled frequency." Some spirits did indeed disappear, though more offended at the oafishness of the functionary in question than swayed by their rational incantations. Those who stayed were starting to lose their patience, and a statistically significant number of functionaries ended up with their entrails decorating the walls. The methodology was not long-lived.

Mr. Bartleby, on the other hand, would plant himself at the possessed location, notepad and pencil in hand, and stoically bear silent witness to the spirit conflict. He'd look all around as every sort of spirit protested, demanding its haunted space. Terrifying wails, blood dripping down walls, syncopated colored vibrations, peptic concerts. Bartleby would simply nod professionally, making a note here or there, never losing focus. Then he'd fold his arms and say:

"Well."

And the spirits' protestations would carry on, gradually intensifying, and then stop, floating or dripping or flashing placidly in anticipation of whatever Bartleby might say, at which point he would continue:

"What we have here is a scheduling conflict."

Bartleby would proceed to draw grids in which he assigned blocks of terror to each spirit.

"*You* may swear from this time to that."

"*You*, meanwhile, may hunker down in the wood slats and haunt until five."

"At five o'clock, *you* may expand to your heart's content, however horrifically you wish."

"*You* have no need to confine yourself to your bloody ectoplasmosis, but consider leaving the walls as you found them for the next spirit."

"*You*, go ahead and shout your prayers, but do it in the attic while they're clearing the children's room for you."

Etcetera.

The functionaries slowly dwindled until there were only a few, the few died off, and finally Bartleby was the only one left. He died like a branch, slowly, bowing imperceptibly, iota by iota, seated at his desk.

It was there that his second, eternal contract began, though this one on the other side of existence.

Bartleby accepted it as naturally as it could be accepted, thanks to the new clarity he'd gained when he became a lost soul.

His supernatural office was an amalgamation of all the offices he'd once occupied, or rather of the various partial glories contained therein back when he'd been a bureaucrat. That coffeepot from such-and-such a time, that photocopier from such-and-such a windfall, that summer the air conditioning finally worked. And the alcoholic effluvium of fresh paper, and the staccatic elegance of click-clacking typewriters all analogging the air.

There he discovered that what he'd thought was a useful and necessary job—the taming of the spirits—had been but a concession, because the spirits had no need for order, or timetables, or rational cohabitation. Their horrors already collated, their rackets harmonized, they'd never needed any system. What they'd needed was him, Bartleby, his ready ears and witness-bearing. But now he was one of them as well as being one for them. Now they scared stiff with greater pleasure than ever, wailed shamelessly, floated from one heaven above to another, shook the foundations of centenary mansions in terror.

Earth might have been abandoned, but the absence of matter had been replaced not only with worms, cobwebs, filth, mold: nature also abhors the absence of animosity and stupefaction. Now all of these stupefactors, hailing from so very many eras, were taking charge, and Bartleby noted how spirits coming from different tragedies crowded together, joining in a single shriek and sometimes, for instance, deciding to get married, only to separate one centenary second later and then remarry a centenary second after that; or the way the celebrated concert of regurgitations was on one occasion performed in every cellar and attic in the city.

Bartleby took note after note after note for the mere pleasure of taking them; as soon as he'd jotted them down, whether in spiritual charcoal or ectoplasmic ink, he tossed them over his shoulder, since he chose not to file them, and the papers floated off forever and ever, as though swimming through water that was not wet.

THE OBJECTS

She could swear she heard her not arrive. That she heard her void within the noises of the night, the sirens, the cogwheels, the high-voltage cables, the trucks moving garbage here and there; within the master objects, the messed-up objects, and the stupid objects. Before opening her eyes, but already vigilant, she knew her man wasn't in bed either. She'd sensed him getting up sometime after hearing her daughter's absence.

She focused some more, lying face-up, and then got out of bed to find out. The streets were empty. She could tell by the decisive uproar reaching her from out there. There was nobody, out there. Only the pulseless movement of the objects; the indifferent bustle of the objects, the imperturbable stridency of the objects: no soft bodies to muffle it, is what Velia heard from her bed.

She got up and searched the cubicle that she and the man shared, and the cubicle where they ate with the daughter, and the tiny cubicle where she was now listening to her daughter's absence.

Velia didn't want to admit it, but she was scared. Not scared of her daughter not being there but of her absence being so palpable. She tried not to sense the girl, tried to set her aside like a silly sense of foreboding. Then she thought of the man. The man would be out looking for her, no doubt, but suddenly Velia felt she had no idea about him either, that at that moment she knew nothing at all of his whereabouts. And she always knew something, the way you know, without looking, what's on the underside of a table. That was the way she always knew about the man. Yet now it was as though the underside of the table were but a hole.

She decided to shake herself off from the inside out, like a wet dog, disperse the stress from within.

She put on her boots and round-brimmed hat, threw her shawl over her shoulders, and let it spill down the length of her body like an instant tan. Then Velia switched on her Miniminder. She synced it to her daughter's and the man's; she waited, waited, waited, waited. Her daughter appeared, a red dot on the screen, he appeared a minute later, a black dot in the same vicinity, both moving farther from Velia. She didn't know their exact location but her Miniminder placed them in a specific vicinity. Better than nothing.

Velia went out and saw the desiccated world. No sign of secretions. Blood, yes, but just traces, as ever, a few drops under a car's engine, a splash on a wall, a red shoe print or tire mark, always dry. A silence of organs and a systematic ruction of objects.

A train that seemed to be traveling at impossibly great speed past the condominiums' windows, automated cranes, automated drills, cables along which incandescent black boxes glided, a cold buzzing.

Velia looked at her Miniminder and began walking in the direction indicated. She turned down one street, took an avenue identical to the one before, rounded a corner, then another, all the same in their rectilinear resolve except one, on which halfway down there stood a building sort of gnawed-up from within, a building with something sucking down the floor from below. Velia was slowly getting closer to the two points, which did not stop and in turn seemed to be getting closer and then farther from each other. On the map she saw there was a more or less direct route: if she picked up the pace she could get within shouting distance of one of them, but when she turned onto the street that would bring her close, her Miniminder started vibrating and the route turned electric orange, indicating impassable traffic. Velia chose to ignore it, and the Miniminder changed from orange to flamboyant yellow and vibrated when a Highly Dangerous Route notification appeared. She turned around and, after taking the recommended detour, her Miniminder piped down.

Velia began walking fast, faster and faster, to make up for the bypass she was being sent on. After a few blocks she began to run. Running made her feel she was making up time, concentrating on her breath, on the sweat trickling down her head and armpits: her little organic atmosphere in the conglomeration of objects. And helped her not think too much, or not think in a particular way, the dubious way, or, worse yet, the ominous intuition way, not think about the where, the what, the what-if.

For a moment she felt almost happy, felt she was achieving something, until her Miniminder lit up in purple, warning her she'd have to stop running. Danger of Trampling, it said. Velia didn't see who she might trample, or who might trample her, but since the Miniminder began vibrating uncontrollably, she slowed her pace. Both dots, which for one iota had seemed promisingly close, grew farther once more.

She was moving so slowly that two stupid objects caught up to and then passed her; two aerosol cans, not on wheels, not floating, were being swept along the concrete by who knows what; no sooner had they passed than they stopped and turned to Velia, or rotated their nozzles to her, as though questioning her, but since they were stupid, they were simply there. A little farther on, an improbable insect clumsily crossed the street, and one of the stupid cans turned and followed it. The other continued before Velia and sprayed a little of whatever it had to spray in her direction, but it was just a bit of nothing, a few drops that didn't even make it the few iotas separating them. Then it turned and followed the other stupid can.

A truck passed, picking up any organic waste and all pieces of objects that weren't fulfilling some specific function, even a stupid function. It stopped, swept, suctioned, pincered, compressed. Almost as though it were accompanying Velia while pretending not to notice her. Velia didn't like hearing it travel beside her. She turned at the next corner, and then the next, trying both to get away from the truck and to get close to the dots on the screen.

But the warnings began to multiply. DON'T TAKE THAT ROUTE:

Road Blocked.

Street Under Automated Maintenance.

Outbreak of Unspecified Violence.

Landslide Zone.

Climatological Anomaly.

Objects Working.

She spent some time thus, ricocheting from one corner to another, then finally stood still in the middle of a street. Only then did her Miniminder stop vibrating and admonishing. Velia assumed she would soon receive some sign alerting her that a new route had opened up.

She stared and stared at her screen but no authorization appeared. Meanwhile the two dots kept getting farther apart, now moving in opposite directions, steadily farther, farther and farther, farther and farther. Velia thought of her daughter and her man while watching the two dots: for a moment she saw them moving, not as dots but the way the living move: her daughter's swaying hair, the little sun-creases in the back of her man's neck.

Before they disappeared from the screen entirely, she heard the electric buzz of the garbage truck, lingering, just behind her.

THE OBJECTS

Every night Rafa stares at the vestibule in hatred until those in line protest. Then he crosses it and is transformed.

But sometimes, no matter how much we pressure him, he keeps staring at the vestibule as though his scowl could destroy it. Last night before entering he turned to me and said:

"I can't stand it."

I know, we all know. But Rafa, he can't adjust.

I pointed to one of my ears and said:

"Wait for me on the other side."

He entered the vestibule. I closed those eyes, while I still had them, and followed: a fleeting gelatinousness, a flash of disintegration. Then I emerged from the building transformed into a rat. The moment I felt Rafa-louse jump onto my ear I started to run, before anyone from the upper offices appeared transformed into a dog or cat. And because that's how I cope. Run, run, run, scurry along pipes, climb walls, inhabit my new body by running. Then eat. That's what we come out for. I let Rafa feed off me, but I myself search for food scraps discarded who knows when or by whom. Detritus. Delicacy. When you're a pestilent creature, the world is no longer pestilent.

After that I start greeting the others. So to speak. I say,

inwardly, when I bump into another scourge, "That you, so-and-so? Looking good today, so-and-so." And I laugh. Inwardly. After crossing the vestibule, a rat is a rat is a rat, even if at times it's still capable of people-reasoning.

Then I go back to ratting. Rats can't concentrate on anything.

After that I sleep (that's what we go out for) in a basement warmed by a mechanical afterthrum. This time I dreamed sounds: footsteps on upper floors, eyes shutting with a snap. There are no words in rat dreams, only residues of lives you more or less remember.

"What do you think the higher-ups are transformed into?" Rafa asked. "What other *thing* could they be?"

I say nothing. Rafa says one day he's going to go up and find out. We already know those right above us are transformed into cats and dogs. I imagine those at the very top are transformed into lions or elephants. Or sharks. Maybe when they emerge from their vestibule, crystal clear pools await and they swim all night and then cross back at dawn. From below all we can see are enormous balconies.

Dawn. Before returning to the building I climb a desiccated tree or a pile of debris to watch the day dawn. I sprawl snout-out in the sun and watch it rise as it warms my claws. Today for a moment I remembered why day used to be called *all the blessed day*. Then I went back to the building to spend all the dark day at work until it was time to cross the vestibule once more.

I didn't see Rafa when I got back. Not the first time it's happened. He's often so anxious to stop being a louse that as soon as he crosses back he immediately dons his work coveralls so he can be a person as long as possible. Regardless, he'll have to undress and go through the vestibule again sooner or later (even those who manage to do double shifts have to sleep and eat occasionally).

At break time I went to find him. On the floor immediately above they gave me a scornful look, perhaps because they've owed me a raise, to squirrel at the very least, for quite some time. Still, I asked if anyone had seen him. No one replied. Until I said loudly:

"Ask you to speak and you won't speak, as though you had the option whenever you wanted."

Then one of them stood up, said:

"Maybe you haven't heard, but despite our best efforts to prevent it, the building is falling down, there's less and less space, so who knows—maybe they didn't let your little friend back in."

He was smiling. Smiling a lips-only smile. Like the animal he was outside, perhaps.

I couldn't find Rafa.

At the end of the day, when everyone started heading to the vestibules, I went upstairs again, not to the next floor up this time but higher and higher: more and more stairs, emptier and emptier. For the last few flights I saw no one at all, and the top floor was equally deserted. There were no guards, only a frosty solitude like a giant sign saying I shouldn't be there. I walked through increasingly dim storerooms. And then I thought I heard something, a click, a clack, one hollow sound and then another. So I said:

"Rafa."

I don't know why. Or I do. Because it was the one remaining possibility, if he hadn't stayed outside. That he was there, among the carnivores.

The sounds were crystal clear now, coming from a storeroom, where finally light could be seen coming in from behind the door closing it off.

I opened it and saw not a soul. And saw not a *soul*. Only an ocean of objects in silence. Suddenly I heard the clack I'd heard before and, from the corner of my eye, saw one of them fall, pushed from the other side of the vestibule: an armchair or a pane of glass or a hatchet, doesn't matter. Another object, in from the outside, and then, on one side of the vestibule, Rafa, crouched down, head between his thighs, waiting for the moment to start his new job and push the bosses out of the building.

FLAT MAP

Perhaps they could have saved the lives of all those who died chasing the truth to the ends of the earth if they'd thought more about, say, the density of trees. But these people, like all people, felt compelled to see things with their own eyes, which would later be eaten by the fish.

And then they went and felled a tree and were confronted with a fleeting yet insufficiently revelatory shock: it was not an immense, uneven wall of tree impossible to circumvent, but individual trees that ended, and behind these trees were others, and with their wood they built wagons to reach the sea, and at the seashore they built boats and even decent-sized ships. And they set sail to see if, as they believed, the horizon would curve at some point, allowing them to circle the earth; but they never returned.

Until one day one of them managed to return to tell the tale, because he'd gone right behind the main ship in another ship to help out, if there was a way to do so. He said they'd sailed for a long long time, covering countless cycles of iotas: iotas and iotas and more iotas, and that just as they were about to abandon the enterprise they finally reached the end of the earth. But he said they didn't realize it until the lead boat was already there, literally one iota from the abyss.

And that one of the men on the ship that was disappearing bow-first over the edge was running in the opposite direction from the abyss and managed to say from the stern, before they saw a scaly tail appear and before the man himself was turned into nothing but an iota.

"Dragons! They're dragons!"

THE EARTHLING

It took a few seconds for him to process the significance of what he'd seen. And by the time he did, it had already disappeared.

He didn't know what it was. A countenance. No. A gesticulation. No: just an irregularity in the landscape, he couldn't say what kind. But he knew that the thing that had briefly flashed across his field of vision had come from Earth. Nothing in this world moved like that, at that speed, with that cadence. So what was it?

An earthling. Martians didn't take walks. They walked slowly but with purpose; when they stopped it was to learn the news by peering carefully around: they'd blink those beautiful translucid eyelids and then keep walking, always at the same pace.

An earthling. He felt his heart surge violently. While he was on Earth, even after the Earth had begun to empty out, hearing "We have someone in common" was not unusual. Everyone had come across, or intercrossed, or crossed everyone else, so they were all superficially or genealogically or rancorously related. Now he had nobody in common with anybody. Now he was alone.

Or not.

He held his chest as if it were about to break open. But he couldn't just drop everything to set off in search of the earthling.

He had to work. The Martians were starting to give him strange looks. *Strange looks* was the best he could do to describe the Martians' facial expressions. Whereas on Earth faces told of desires and of battles lost, faces here were walled off. He could make out a few nuances but they appeared and disappeared so imperceptibly as to be almost undetectable to him.

They weren't Martians, of course, and he was not on Mars. Who knew where he was? But he had to call them something, because when he'd tried to find out the name of the planet and what they called themselves, they hadn't understood the question.

They were giving him strange looks: he should have been working by that time. All Martians knew—intuited?—what work each of them had to do. It would be no use trying to explain to them that he needed to do something really important, something unputoffable. Martians were never in a hurry.

It was a busy day, there were lots of Martians moving in, and the wires that carried power to their new houses moved with them. On Mars there were no overhead cables, Martians didn't grid up their space with cables, or city blocks, or furrows (which is why, when he'd arrived, the man had assumed he would find no civilization). A spontaneous wire structure transported energy to wherever there were people. The wires twined together in the ground in the manner of roots, and he had to amend their configuration each day. They'd discovered he had a talent for this task. Maybe that was their way of telling him what they called themselves: the way we move, that's our name.

But today he paid no attention to the way the Martians and their wires were moving; he kept looking up, hoping to see that presence return.

At more or less the muggy time of day, he realized something was going on. The Martians had interrupted their journeys and were absorbed in the news they were slowly assimilating from their surroundings. What happened? he asked. Having just learned to read the environment himself, he had to wait for one of them to inform him that a volcano had erupted on the other side of the planet. The Martian had learned this by beholding the clouds. Another one determined, from the way the shadows fell, the precise location.

If what he'd seen was news, it was so only to him.

The following day he discovered nothing new. After work he went to speak to a Martian he thought was the closest thing to a government official. On Mars there were no government offices. On Mars the state is more like a series of understandings than a series of books or desks. It's the regularity of rituals, tacit rules, scarcely gesticulated negotiations. This Martian in particular spent his days sitting on a rock reading the environment, becoming informed about everything without restricting his center of interest to any particular place.

"Something happened yesterday, something that concerns me," he said. "I need information."

The Martian stared at him, blinked, but showed no sign of having anything to say in response.

"Can you tell me what it's about?"

The Martian pointed to some bushes.

"The volcano stopped spewing lava," he said.

"I'm not talking about the volcano," he responded. "I'm talking about something else."

The Martian closed his eyes and squinted ever so slightly, as though making no more than a little-baby effort.

"Someone who lives not far from here had a terrible night, something disrupted their sleep."

"I'm not talking about someone who slept poorly, I'm talking about something that concerns me directly, but I don't know what it is," he insisted.

A few seconds passed in silence before he added:

"I know *that* concerns me directly as well, but I'm talking about something else."

"I see," said the Martian. And stopped paying him any attention.

For several days he tried to find out if anyone else had seen whatever it was, but the Martians scarcely gave him a passing look before going back to their business. He carried on with his routine of following the wires, drawing them, handing in his diagrams each day, but didn't stop attempting to locate whatever it was that he didn't know *what* it was but was certain *that* it was. Once in a while he'd be gripped by fear or desperation that he fought off by summoning the clarity of whatever it was against the Martian landscape.

He'd seen it. Just *glimpsed* it, true. But he hadn't imagined it.

He hadn't seen that disruption in the landscape again. After a few weeks he began to resign himself, but it was a sadder kind of resignation than he was used to suffering.

One day he came upon a group of kids he'd seen before, always together and always silent. Martian children spoke little, and when they did, it was in complete, complex sentences. That's why he was amazed when one of them, the smallest of the gang, elongated his neck and said:

"A message came who walks like you."

He stared at the child, waiting for him to say something else, but the whole gang turned in unison and left.

He kept walking toward his house and on the way began to notice that the Martians were stopping to look at him, a few even with the hint of something resembling a smile. The boy had said "a message came who walks," which made no sense; perhaps he'd misunderstood, maybe the kid had said "a *messenger* came." He sped up, and even if he was scratching the Martian landscape with his agitation, nobody gave him a strange look. He felt almost as if a Martian might clap him on the back, if they knew how.

He was no longer walking toward his house but was still walking decisively. He was reading the environment and would speed up or suddenly turn without thinking about where he was going. He understood that this was the way Martians guided themselves, and that his steps were taking him to the earthling. Finally, finally, finally. Finally he was going to find the earthling. They were going to talk. They were going to talk and this other person would tell him how he got there, and they'd find a way out or at least find a way to make being there more bearable.

And then he saw the earthling.

And the earthling saw him too and began running toward him, jumping excitedly, and on reaching him leapt up on his hind legs, licked his face, rubbed his head against his chest, and wagged his tail from side to side.

And he, in a single vertiginous second, experienced a series of emotions he thought had been left back on the old planet: astonishment, intense sorrow, and then uncontainable joy because, after all, he'd found the earthling.

THE MONSTERS' ART

"We need the monsters' art," he said, and produced an official document mandating as much.

The bailiff swept his eyes slowly over the document, as though assessing its gravity, but he wasn't assessing it, just giving the impression of doing so.

"Of course," he said. And turned.

He pushed open the wooden door now in front of him and walked into the next room, showed the document to the secretary, who solemnly swept his eyes over it and nodded, then walked to the back of the room, turned the knob of the second door, which was plastic. In the next room was nothing but a desk with a single drawer. He opened the drawer and extracted a ring of three keys, used one to open the next door, the aluminum door, and walked into the next room. Nothing in it, just silvery metal walls. He used the two remaining keys to open the next door, which had an oak finish but a soul of steel, and entered the last room. This one was also all metal but littler than the others. The ceiling was a single square bulb, which illuminated one shelf holding bottles and another shelf on which lay a blunt-tipped cane and a box containing rolls of paper of various textures; on the floor was a square black device with a cord, also black. He placed one bottle, the cane, and a roll of paper on top of the apparatus and pushed the whole of it to the next door, which resembled that of a safe. The bailiff spun the dial on the combination lock this way, then that, then this again, this again, this, that, spanning the segments of each revolution with expertise, tempo, and determination until the lock went *click*. Then he pulled the titanium-handled hatch and entered the monsters' room.

By the entrance, hanging from a nail, was a clipboard with a paper with squares to be ticked off. The bailiff made three ticks on as many lines, turned, took the cane, turned the handle, and entered the first monster's dungeon. He caught the monster making art. Banging and banging its hairy fists against a sheet of sepia paper that had been marked up in distressing fashion on the concrete floor. Catching the monster making art was extremely difficult, as the monster was timid, but it didn't mind being seen making monstrosities, for which they provided all required supplies. There was no one left in the dungeon, just shreds of clothing and shards of bone; maybe that was why, with no one to manhandle, it had begun making art.

The monster turned to the bailiff, stunned and slobber-mouthed, and tensed its muscles, preparing to pounce and tear him to pieces, but by then the bailiff was wielding the cane and whacked it down on the monster's back until he felt it go soft and then on the monster's skull until he felt it go soft and then on the monster's extremities until he felt them rendered useless and only then did he approach to examine the art on the floor; fortunately, the art had been spattered with blood. He picked it up, left another piece of paper in its place, and walked out.

The bailiff slid the monster's art into a cardboard tube, tucked the bottle into the waistband of his trousers, and moved on to dungeon number two. The monster in this dungeon was expect-

ing him. It was curled up in a corner, hurling a litany of hatred
with its gaze, almost as if speaking with its eyes. The litany grew
louder and louder and the monster began unfurling from the
corner toward the bailiff, as though its bones were slow springs,
and brought its nose right up to the bailiff's, a nothing away. The
bailiff was frightened but remembered his training: he must not
let himself be intimidated by the litany or by the monster's un-
folding bones, so he brandished the cane and crashed it down,
shattering an eye socket. No problem; they healed. Then he shat-
tered its mouth, and once the monster had curled back up, he
pushed it in order to collect what the monster was hiding, but the
monster turned its back on the bailiff and held on, refusing to let
go, so the bailiff began striking its claws until it finally let go and
the bailiff was able to pick up the bundle, which was a doll rep-
resenting something, a girl or a cat, something with huge, smiley
eyes. He took the bottle from his trousers, opened it, sprayed
firewater onto the monster's wounds, and then threw it the bottle,
which the monster rushed to pick up and bring to its mouth.

He placed the doll and the tube by the door to the monsters'
ward, hooked up the square contraption, and nudged it along.
Before entering the third dungeon, he turned the thing on and
a series of lights on the rim of the box blinked. He bent over it,
pressed a concealed button on the top, and said, "Testing, testing," pressed another button and heard himself speak, and nodded
in satisfaction. As soon as the bailiff stepped into the dungeon,
the monster began to wail. The bailiff carried the box in with
him and the monster's wails became more desperate. It was small
and misshapen, with some extremities shorter than others. The
monster used them all to bury its nails into its skin and injure itself and began to expel various secretions—brown, yellow—from
its orifices.

"No, no, stop that," said the bailiff, attempting to approach the monster, the cane in one hand, pushing the black box with the other. "Don't do that."

But the monster wouldn't stop spraying him with its nauseating secretions. It was no longer making any sound and instead was focused on making more and more pus-secreting wounds, until the bailiff began to strike strategic blows with the cane, first on its extremities, and then, since the monster only moaned crossly, on its chest and genitals. Then the monster really did let out a sound that was first deep and low, then sweet and almost sharp, and all the while blue. The bailiff pressed the button on the box and, when he noticed that it had stopped singing, struck the monster again and it sang again, in great pain and in a great range of keys; at one point the bailiff even began tapping his foot in time, until the monster seemed to falter irremediably and stop secreting and stop singing and turned into a useless blob.

The bailiff exited the dungeon, put the other pieces of art atop the recording box, and exited the monsters' ward.

He went back through the shock-absorbing rooms, making sure to lock each one carefully. In the penultimate room, the secretary made note of the art he was removing before finally returning to reception.

The messenger waited in mute impatience. He made no gesture or comment about the filth covering the bailiff. He took the monsters' art, turned, and walked off.

The bailiff looked down to record the removal in the day's logbook before going off to change. As he did so he began biting a nail and, without realizing it, kept going until he noticed he was gnawing the bone. He stood staring at the naked tip of his phalanx and only then did he feel a stab of pain, though flesh was already beginning to cover the bone once more. The bailiff began to cry. Not because it hurt but because of all the times he'd eaten his own flesh and told himself that he too had what it took to make art.

OBVERSE

And that was why they decided to go off and explore the other side, on which, they hoped, there would be no watery cliffs or dragons awaiting them at the end.

They traversed iotas and iotas. Deserts of iotas and dales of iotas and mountains of iotas. Millions of iotas. Until, finally, once again, they reached a place where there were no more iotas to traverse but another cliff, an earth cliff. And they began to rappel between its cascading crags, which rushed past in more of a rush than they were in to discover what was below. What *was* below? Long, long roots extending for iotas and iotas from the feet of the trees of the world? A hard, impenetrable rock supporting the world? Flocks flapping their wings continuously to hold up the world?

Vast numbers of explorers were lost in a descent that took decades, which are vast accumulations of iotas of time: iotas and iotas of beats. Finally, some reached the bottom of the cliff, their bodies bearing the consequences of such a long deprivation: ever-so-bearded, ever-so-filthy, fingernails ever-so-long, layers of earth covering what were once coats and shirts and skin. And when they arrived they discovered that on the other side there was no need to hold on to the wall and they could plant their feet because the world was also solid, and had light, not eternal darkness, as they'd believed, and there were also plants and creatures and trees just like on the other side, and even people: people on a day trip sitting around a blanket, who on seeing the explorers had widened their eyes, just a bit at first, barely an iota, and then wider and then inordinately wide, and they'd shouted in terror: "Dragons! They're dragons!"

INVENTORY OF HUMAN DIVERSITY

For my nephew Tonita Herrera Pizarro

Appendix 87: Inventory of Human Diversity
          This appendix catalogs all varieties of human
          beings in existence.
          Number of specimens: 1

Potocki slammed shut his notebook. He had no need to reread the description of the animal before him. Didn't know why he even bothered to check the appendix every day, since all it did was rile him up. Maybe that was why: to avoid becoming resigned to the mediocre, dead-end job he was stuck in.

Oh, how those oafs at the Terrarium must have laughed. In other departments they actually had variety, healthy specimens, interns, budgets. They did experiments, published the results, attended conferences. The Terrarium contained multiple specimens of every species on the planet, specimens with trunks and specimens with gills, specimens they'd found in trees and specimens they'd found slithering along. Meanwhile Potocki did nothing but take note of the steady decline of the only human specimen they had. Guy spent all day huddled in a corner of his cage and no longer complained via sporadic, incomprehensible sounds that Potocki had first thought were a language but now suspected were nothing but an externalization of his health, like a rash on one's skin or a secretion. It couldn't be a language: languages were used to communicate. And this human was utterly alone.

That was the key. Maybe if he succeeded in getting the human to communicate, Potocki would be able to learn more about him. But how could he, when the bureaucrats from the Collections division had fumigated the entire planet before verifying that they had preserved at least two of each species? Bunch of peabrains.

What he needed to do, as they'd said on the initial induction course, was think outside the box. Outside the box. Outside the box. Learn to create synergies, they'd insisted over and over. Well, he'd flipping love to create synergies, if anyone at the damned zoo was willing to help him.

And then he thought outside the box. Those bigheads at the Terrarium were the box. Potocki got so happy realizing what he had to do that he went to feed the human again, even though he'd already had his daily rations.

That night he waited in his little office for everyone to leave and then took a spin through the Terrarium. He knew there were several possible solutions to the problem. He moseyed through the area with the air beasts, the water beasts, the land beasts, the underground beasts, and the beasts that soared over the earth. He headed to the tree beast area.

He found his specimen—healthy, glorious. He took him down with an anesthetic and carted him in a wheelbarrow back to his section.

Before sticking the beast in the human's cage, Potocki reveled for a few seconds, thinking of how happy the human would be. Because who cared if those holier-than-thous from Taxonomy had given them different names? To him they looked like basically the same species, one hairier than the other, one far stronger and more aggressive than the other, true, but aside from that they were practically identical, orangutans and humans.

He opened the human's cage, wheeled in the wheelbarrow with the orangutan, and left it there. The human threw himself against the wall, staring at the other specimen, eyes wide. Surprised, no doubt. But how happy the human would be when the orangutan awoke. If all went well, soon he'd have a new specimen to show off. A specimen that could *speak*. He could picture the faces of his colleagues at the Terrarium, just see if they dared to repeat that humans were expendable.

ZORG, AUTHOR OF THE QUIXOTE

When he wasn't rapturously touching his own tet, Zorg was inventing stories about improbable worlds. It had been only seventy-five years since he'd left the nest of his mothers and fathers and tothers, to the great delight of all seven of them, and since then he'd made the most of the privacy afforded by his private lair to touch himself rapturously; more than astonishing moves he'd never before made with his claw, what was most wonderful was the freedom with which he could take his carapace off in any room he liked and touch his tet and discover new possibilities over time, which was all people like Zorg, with only five or six tet, had (Zorg claimed to have seven but in fact had only six). Such passion for the possibilities offered up by existence was what led him to start inventing stories, some about the people he knew, who were few; most about people who might one day exist, though most likely not.

Eventually, Zorg set out into the world for the second time. He began, as the saying goes, to get some air in light of his tet. Interacting was far easier than he'd imagined during his early years of confinement. He befriended people with all manner and number of tet, diligently finding the factorial with them all.

But there was one who inspired in him a desire for something more: he longed to sit in silence with her, longed for them to tease each other, for them to sing cheery little songs to each other and, if need be, nice little songs of solace. Pirg had nineteen tets, each with different gifts. With Zorg she'd shared only seven, motivated by a precise sense of symmetry. "You have to earn the rest." Yet that wasn't the only reason he loved Pirg; he loved her also because she was able to appreciate the importance of stories, especially new or re-newed stories. Pirg worked in a story-incubator lair, but it took a long time before Zorg was willing to show her one of his. He was hiding behind their nice little songs and shared rapture.

And yet one day he decided to show her the stories he'd spent a few decades working on. They were few but they were his. Zorg wrote stories about fantastical beings trapped in one way or another by bodily limitations, geographical limitations, epistemological limitations: people who were always doing battle and almost always losing but who from time to time managed to break through those limitations and then beautiful things occurred. It was all a little corny. Though he'd also written the story of three characters who were headed to a kind of temple in order to heal one of them, and to get to this temple they had to cross a desert rife with temptations (Zorg still laughed with pleasure on thinking of the "temptations" concept), and along the way one of the characters decided to exchange the character they were partnered with for the other. Each had only one tet, thus the decision for them to be with only one person. It was a perfectly rational decision, and in the end they all suffered. Dramatic!

He'd also written the story of some itty-bitty beings who discovered the best way to grow, inside some pillows on which other, more vulnerable beings lay their heads to sleep without realizing they were but a resource for the survival of the other, smaller, yet more evolved beings. Shocking!

And four or five others.

Pirg generally responded with benevolence, sometimes even with enthusiasm, but never with fake adulation. She even returned a few of his stories with nothing but a Pfeh. This gave Zorg the confidence to show her another story, slightly longer, which he'd been calling the *Quixote*.

"Short title, to the point, punchy," he said to himself as he approached Pirg's lair. He found her editing a story; by her sides a couple were finding the factorial. One worked with Pirg, the other Zorg was pretty sure lived close by. Neither glanced up at him as he entered.

Zorg dropped his claw-written document on Pirg's desk and adopted a triumphal stance, two of his arms akimbo.

"What?" Pirg said, as if annoyed that he'd distracted her from her work, or as if to say, Look at the pair of them, making it impossible to focus.

"This is the story I told you about."

"The one about the guy who goes around and another guy who goes with him and stuff happens to them or something, right? Yeh, yeh, original." She made a dismissive gesture. "Stick it over there."

Zorg didn't stick it over there but instead stuck it right in front of Pirg's eyes, the ones on the front of her head, and waited. Pirg repeated the dismissive gesture but began reading the text he'd clawed out. Very quickly her dismissiveness turned to real concentration. She gave Zorg a surprised little look and said to him:

"Come back in a bit."

And to the two finding the factorial by her sides: "Go on, scram, let me work."

Zorg left Pirg's lair in triumphal spirits, but while he was killing time his anxiety began to grow, and soon he was worried not only about what Pirg would think but about his place in the world and about the finitude of things and the folly of his flesh and particularly about the fact that nothingnothingnothing could remedy any of those lucid nightmares, because, of course, there was also the *in*finitude of things, which made it all worse; then he realized enough time had passed and went back.

Pirg was sprawled on the sofa behind her desk. She watched Zorg enter and gave him the barest hint of a smile as he settled himself opposite her. Pirg said nothing, just watched him in silence, as if she were studying something on Zorg's face, something that she knew must be there but was invisible to the naked eye.

"I don't really know what you were expecting me to say," she finally said. "You know how predictable I find speculative fiction. It's formulaic, it's contrived, it's adolescent."

Zorg began to stammer with both mouth and extremities but Pirg cut him off.

"Still, there's something here we can work with."

She hunched over the desk and began flipping pages.

"Though this isn't serious prose, some of the ideas you've got here are real gems. Others, like having their genitalia limited to two options . . . please. I don't see why you keep going back to that flight of fancy; regardless, I suppose even with those limitations some degree of drama can be developed."

"Significantly more drama," Zorg replied. "It's precisely the scarcity of genital resources that makes employing them even more dramatic."

"Pfeh. Says you. Anyway, what I did think you developed well was Quixote's reasoning for doing what he does—let's come back to his name later. It's so easy to say someone acts a certain way simply because they've been hurt or because they've been called to do so, but then a character is nothing but the noise an object makes when it's touched, and who cares. Your character, on the other hand, concocts his own reasoning. Like when Sancho asks why he's acting all crazy when Dulcinea's given him no cause to be jealous, and Don Quixote says, 'That's the beauty of my plan. If a knight goes crazy for a reason, there is no thanks or value attached to it. The thing is to go crazy *without* a reason, and to make my lady understand that if I do this when dry, what will I do when drenched?'"

Then Pirg laughed. And not her sharp, pfehty laugh, but one of pure joy and shared connection. For a second Zorg considered making the most of it and moving in to find factorials, but he intuited that it might ruin the moment.

"I wasn't expecting this from you, Zorg. Sometimes you seem so basic," she said, confirming that he'd done well to keep his tet in check. "In the same vein, I like the whole windmill thing, sure, since he has to invent a rationale to keep going, but isn't conceiving it as insanity a tad conservative? I mean, wouldn't we expect a decent guy to try to do battle against some monstrosity that's a blight on nature? Anyway, just a thought."

She turned back to the text and began flipping through it as if Zorg weren't there, but Zorg could tell that Pirg was searching for a particular passage.

"I like the subplot with this other character silently commenting on the action throughout. Not so convinced about his appearance, though. Shouldn't Rocinante be like the character you invented in that other story, the 'hippopotamus'?" she said, making claw quotes in the air. "To bear all the stuff he bears, that poor creature has to be really strong."

"I don't think a hippopotamus could survive in the environment where the action takes place. It has to spend almost all day in the water, remember? And this is a far more arid setting."

"Well, then, at least get rid of that horn and floating rainbow, use a little imagination for the love of tet, Zorg. If you're going to invent bodies, don't just blindly replicate the ones you already know."

Zorg felt a mix of shame at having lapsed into cliché and anger that Pirg had pointed it out but managed to appear undaunted, as though in actual fact he wanted to be criticized.

"One part that had me in tears," she went on, pointing to the back of her head where she'd cried, "was when Sancho and Don Quixote find the bandits' limbs hanging from trees. So poignant. Made me think of the tree where three or four of my great-grandparents are hanging . . . Harvest time is nearing."

Pirg stared off into space and Zorg knew not to interrupt her. He too thought of his hanged who would soon be ripe. Such thoughts usually made him want to tet off, but Pirg's was such a delicate silence that he didn't so much as lift a claw.

"Anyway," said Pirg, "that scene really works."

She smiled at him with a new kind of tenderness, and to Zorg's surprise, Pirg reached out an eighth tet under the desk and began finding his factorial. Zorg began to weep through a hidden tear duct that was activated only in moments of chaste emotion.

"It's a great title, right?" Zorg asked after they'd spent a while sweetly finding each other's factorial.

"If you're not going to change the character's name, sure, or if you want the title to focus on that character's actions. Personally, I'd like a more euphonic title, or a less journalisticky one, something like 'Aldonanza Lorenzo's Season of Rest.' Or, since you invented that whole 'journey' concept and your characters can't appear quantically, you could use that somehow. Plus, keep in mind that almost nobody's going to read it, so have a little fun with the title."

"I thought I could add a few spaceships."

"Nice, nice! Anachronism brings it closer to dirty realism. We'll see."

And, spontaneously, they began to sing a sweet song of contentment.

THE OTHER THEORY

After it was confirmed that Earth is indeed flat, a sect was formed. No one knows what they call themselves, only that their name somehow includes allusions to sugar and salt crystals. Their concern is no longer what's on the Other Side; that much has been accepted as Mystery: no one has recommended any sort of expedition since the last one went down the earthen precipice, never to return. This sect maintains—not as their principal dogma but as a secondary deduction, like a given—that whatever's on the other side must undoubtedly be simpler and cruder than what's on this one, the complex side.

Their principal dogma is that if Earth is flat, and if the garden of delights that is the World is a reflection of the same formula on which the rest of the universe is modeled, then Earth must exist for the benefit of something else. Like sustenance. Earth as a host wafer, a tortilla, a cracker traveling through the universe, just awaiting an encounter with the mouth of the Creator. And we are what imparts the flavor. Earth, to them, is concrete proof of divine cosmic pleasure.

A smaller sect within the sect upholds this same dogma but interprets it differently: our ability to see that we are the lone mouthful nobody cares about proves we are nothing; we are not

God's favored creations, nor is there anyone to chew us up; if there's a banquet, that banquet is taking place elsewhere.

We regularly mock the sect's members. Everybody knows that the Creator is not a mouth but the eye of a dragon, and that the world is but a blink, a blink, a blink set to happen: now.

THE CONSPIRATORS

Pel put on her sunglasses without thinking, in an unconscious response to the information that had struck her brain like a teeny bolt of lightning: that she'd need them. Then she went outside. No sooner had she left than a ray of sun hit her squarely as it shone down between two buildings, but since she was wearing the sunglasses, she wasn't blinded and was able to see that one of those silent beasts that pull carts was bearing down on her and had time to get out of the way. There'd been buku accidents involving those beasts. They were tame and strong as all get-out, overfed tardigrades that didn't make a sound, which is why they often trampled dimwitted pedestrians. Pel was able to predict little things; not huge cataclysms or the earth's movements, but this kind of insignificant event was something she could foresee. That was the way her body was adapting to the planet. As far as she knew, it wasn't happening to the rest of them, neither Ones nor the Others, who'd arrived long, long before her, though when they'd left there had been little difference between them. Often, their state of mind would momentarily manifest: some nervous nellie's ears would prick up, or a scaredy-cat would temporarily shrink.

She walked along, apprehensive. Ever since the day of the

secret meeting, Pel had been looking over her shoulder. She strolled aimlessly around a park and, when she was sure no one was following her, headed to the establishment to which Professor Cradoq had summoned her.

Pel found him sitting at a table in a dark corner, where he could see who walked in and out. He had an invigorating pot of soup before him and was plopping in red pebbles to make it less bitter. Cradoq lowered his head just a bit to acknowledge that he'd seen her and that they shouldn't call attention to themselves. Pel approached the table and sat down across from him almost without moving the chair.

"Thanks for coming," said Cradoq.

"Why wouldn't I?" Pel asked. "If you told me to keep quiet that day, it means you're going to tell me everything."

They'd met a few days earlier, at one of those meetings of conspirators who were lacking in resources but brimming with the need to voice their conscience for the sole purpose of receiving validation that they were right. Pel had gone because she went wherever she was invited, and one of the conspirators had invited her after recognizing her from another party that she'd also gone to because she went wherever she was invited. The conspirators were young, except Cradoq, who, judging by his bored expression, might have been hoping for a different kind of get-together. The attendees took turns stating the obvious: that a great majority were oppressed by a rapacious, violent minority. They concurred with one another, finished one another's sentences, nodded.

"They act like nothing had ever been wrong, all those generations," said one conspirator, whose hair curled and straightened as she spoke.

"Bunch of criminals," said another burly conspirator, whose brows bushed as he emphasized each word.

"When are we going to do something about the vaccine?" asked a third, sweat creating a little phosphorescent patina at his hairline.

Pel had stopped paying attention to this grumblefest but the question brought her back.

"What vaccine?"

They looked at her with a touch of pity, or something like charitable tenderness.

"They," said the bushy-browed conspirator, "have been inoculating us with a vaccine."

"What kind of vaccine?"

"Anti-insurrection."

Pel made no gesture. The conspirators interpreted this as disbelief. One of them, whose skin pigmentation had altered slowly as he listened but now, as he spoke, stabilized, said:

"I get your skepticism, but that's exactly what gives them power; it's undetectable. They inoculate everyone and that's what makes us apathetic, or indecisive."

"But how do they do it?"

"Nobody knows."

"The water," said the wavy-haired conspirator.

"Put it in our food," said the brow-bushed conspirator.

"At the hospitals," said the phosphorescing conspirator. "That makes the most sense, it's when we're off our guard, and they can make sure to inoculate everyone except their own."

"Nobody knows," repeated the skin-shifting conspirator.

"But when did they start doing this?"

"Right at the beginning," said the burly one, and his brows bushed even more, out of anger. "Ever since our first contact with them, ten generations ago."

Pel knew part of the story, or part of that part of the story. The Ones and the Others had probably arrived on this planet at the same time but came from different eras on that other one, from radically different mindsets and different degrees of technological sophistication; but since they'd arrived buck naked, without their devices, they had to get by on the skills they had. The story went that the Ones were farmers: peaceful, sedentary, poets, even. And that the Others were crude but clever, that they didn't know how to plow the land but knew how to plow people, because they'd found a way to rebuild their weapons, and they were hunters. The Others had laid waste to the Ones, to their will, but had not eliminated the people themselves, or else no one would be left to sow for them and serve them, but they did impose their language and dominate them by way of blood and stone. The Ones had never rebelled, and slowly their submission had been rewarded until, now, the Ones and the Others were supposedly citizens with equal rights, though the Ones exercised them from the swamp and the Others from skyscrapers.

"But we're not," said the mani-pigmented conspirator. "Just take a look at who rules, who punishes."

"Who allocates," added the now smooth-haired conspirator.

"What little is allocated," said browman.

There followed a series of statements that attempted to explain how they knew what they knew, but since nobody knew any details, all they did was pile speculation atop speculation. As if someone in high command had deserted and was collaborating with the opposition, as if a One had worked close to the Others' high command and had heard them gloating over their infallible wonder weapon. As if there were industrial plants on the other side of the planet where they prepared the vaccines and at night shipped them to this side.

In the short time Pel had been on the planet, she'd picked up on the gestures, habits, and reflexes of the Ones and the Others. The muffled rage of the Ones, the arrogance of the Others, who thought they deserved all the privileges they'd been born with.

Pel's time on Earth had briefly coincided with the Others', and there was something about this whole story that didn't add up, something she felt should be there if it was all true—and yet it wasn't.

"I'm sorry, something's not adding up."

All eyes, brows, hairs, and skins were on her, and all ears auricled around toward her, but then Pel noticed that not all the conspirators were paying her the same attention, that there were two who were paying *even more* attention, though a different kind of attention. She focused on only one, because more than attention, it was like an unspoken cry: Professor Cradoq, who hadn't opened his mouth or pigmented his skin or anything of the sort, was pulsing slightly at the top of his hands, a hazy pulsation that didn't quite dare to emerge, but Pel sensed its significance.

"I forgot what I was going to say." And she giggled dopily.

Then she felt everyone relax and at the same time felt someone at the table go on alert but she couldn't tell who.

When the meeting was over, Pel said goodbye to everyone and everyone said goodbye to Pel except for Cradoq, who almost trampled her on his way out. What others would have seen as evidence of insolence, Pel saw as simply a lapse in attention, then almost immediately understood that his snub was a kind of sign. When she was some way from the meeting spot, she patted the pockets on her overalls and, indeed, found in one of them a piece of paper with some elegantly detailed hieroglyphics that read:

Don't talk about that yet.

Let's meet tomorrow at such-and-such time at such-and-such establishment.

Pel gestured at Cradoq's soup and pebbles to tell the waiter she wanted the same, but with her thumb and index finger indicated that she wanted a small, in a little cup. The waiter went off, and

Cradoq and Pel concentrated on each other: an attention bubble that could be felt invisibly ensphering them.

"I'd heard about you, the new arrival—I finally get to meet you."

"I, on the other hand, knew nothing of you, Professor, but I've done my research. You study the life of languages."

"And their afterlives, when I can."

"What were you doing at that meeting? You didn't seem particularly interested."

"I was interested, but not so much in what they were saying; I already know all that. They invite me not to listen to me speak but to listen to each other with a witness present, someone to validate them. They're good people, a few of them were my students, they're intelligent but don't really know where to go with this, aside from pointing out the obvious."

"And is what's happening obvious?"

"Oh, sure, we're governed by satraps, that much is clear. But sometimes all you can do is point it out, since there isn't much else to do. Or at least that's what we've gotten used to."

"So it's true. The Others have the population inoculated."

Cradoq circled the pot with his hands. He was thinking. An ever-so-light, ever-so-white smoke began to emanate from his fingertips, dissolving almost as soon as it hit the air.

"Let's say that it is."

"But how is it possible that no one knows how they do it?"

"We do know. Or, at least, I do."

Pel started to say something but at that moment the waiter arrived with her cup of soup and pebbles. Though Pel hadn't asked for one, the waiter brought her a menu. Pel pretended to scan the hieroglyphics on the card and returned it to him, but the waiter stood there a moment before leaving Pel and Cradoq's bubble. Cradoq watched him with his head bowed, as if counting his pebbles, and not until he saw the waiter enter the kitchen did he say:

"But we need proof." He stacked some coins on the table and said: "Let's go."

"We need proof?" asked Pel, standing. "What changed?"

"You turned up."

They walked for a long time, in silence and erratically, until Cradoq picked up the pace and set a course and they went out to the suburbs and came to an archaeological area that no one paid attention to anymore.

"This is the place where the Ones and the Others first encountered one and other. Or so the story goes."

"Which story?"

"The official one."

"But you all have another version, right?"

"Same version, just deader and more disgraced."

Cradoq told her the story, explaining the subtleties and interests of each side—not just the rabid fragments and the justifications that Pel already knew but also the holes in the story. Nobody really, truly knew who got there first. They did know, of course, that the Ones came from an earlier era, one in which they'd tried to reach an agreement in order to rescue what was left of Earth, and that the Others came from a later era, in which their concern had become the sheer will to survive and the eradication of the doubtful. They'd met here, and after a little friction and a little desertion had recognized one another as travelers from the same place, even if time had made it look like two different places, and they'd learned, the Ones from the Others and the Others from the Ones, and then the Others ended up in charge because they were the ones who were best prepared for a world that had to be subdued.

"The one version, of course, insists that there was no learning and only imposition, plunder, and subjugation. That all that was left of the Ones was their bodies, and that was only to force us to do the drudgery and grunt work of the Others."

Cradoq lowered one knee to the ground and crossed his hands over the other. For a minute it looked to Pel as though he himself were part of the ruins, but whereas the ruins were just parts of columns and grass-covered walls, Cradoq was once again releasing white smoke through his fingertips as he thought.

"What some of us believe," he said finally, "is that the plunder and imposition were far greater even than we'd lamented, and different from what we've always denounced, much more perverse."

Just then Pel was visited by another of her lightning-bolt visions: not only the image but the emotion of a dilated pupil, though she said nothing at first. Then she asked:

"And they did this with that vaccine they were talking about?"

Cradoq's hands emitted a denser smoke that was then sucked back in, as though inhaled.

"What were you going to say didn't add up?"

Pel took a beat to remember what Cradoq meant.

"Oh, that. Well, it's just that I met the Others before, or at least some ones who looked like these Others, but they didn't talk like the Others, they talked different."

"That's something I've suspected for quite some time, but I needed someone who could prove it."

"Prove what?"

"That the Others took not just our land but *our language*, and the world we'd imagined and constructed with that language. Doesn't it seem odd that it's like there's two ways to live together? One by the laws that are imposed and one by the laws of the wild, so to speak?"

"The way the Others have of putting language on and taking it off, like a costume?"

"Yes. What I think is that when they met, the Others saw that the Ones already had an entire network, a form of self-organization, of understanding this planet, and they realized that the best they could do was make the most of it."

"You mean . . ."

"They made our language theirs, said it was theirs and always had been, and then imposed it on us so we'd forget that it had been ours, turned it into a broad brush to paint us in whatever way they pleased. And we forgot it. We forgot that it had been ours and had to relearn it *through them*."

"The vaccine."

"The vaccine. But the vaccine is our story, the one we tell ourselves to justify generation upon generation of submissiveness. The truth is that some of us have lived comfortable lives in submission."

Cradoq's fingertips were stock-still but kind of combusting.

"But stories create truth, no matter how untrue they may be. Now you can help with that truth."

"Telling your truth?"

"No, troubling the Others' truth. Making sure they themselves call it into question. If we do it, no one is going to believe us, not even our side."

Pel was moved. She had never asked if she could collaborate with the Ones and not the Others, but just like that it seemed the most natural thing, not only because she felt like they were children discovering the world, but because she was taken with the idea of being part of a struggle.

"Tell me how."

"How well do you remember that language?"

"Pretty well."

"We need someone, *one of them*, to start spreading the rumor that their language is in fact ours. Plenty of people will start making connections and searching for signs of that other language that almost disappeared. There are still random nouns out there, adjectives nobody understands. And I hope that this someone will be one who attended conspiracy meetings, even though I know he works for the Others."

"A traitor."

"No, he's not a traitor if he lies to us but actually has always worked for them. What I hope is to convince him to become a traitor."

At that moment they heard footsteps and Pel saw, coming down the path from the main road, the man with the moody brows.

"We were just talking about you. Thanks for coming," said Cradoq.

"The origin of all our misfortune, eh?" he asked, eyebrows unmoving, practically sparse. "This is getting interesting."

"It's going to get even more interesting, so much so that in the end you'll be saying 'our misfortune' and it'll mean something else."

The man looked intrigued and Pel saw the way he struggled to keep his brows from sprouting multiple bristles; they'd start to peek out and then pop back in. Cradoq spoke again:

"Pel, please tell me, in the language of the ancestors of this man here, how do you say what we call *real-world sadness*?"

"Treason."

"And how do you say what we call *intermixing*?"

"Atonement."

"And how do you say *interpretation*?"

"Appropriation."

"And how do you say *method*?"

"Big stick."

The man raised one hand almost imperceptibly, as if unintentionally asking Pel to stop. He turned away briefly. Then turned back to them, looking like he'd understood.

"How did you find me out? They chose me specifically because I look like you all."

"That whole business about the physiognomy of One or the Other is sheer storytalk, or at least it hasn't mattered for a long time. I discovered you because you paid attention. At those meetings people listen only to themselves. And then one day I followed you and discovered you talking to your bosses."

"But what good will this knowledge do? Best-case scenario, they'll realize they've been living a lie."

"I think that's exactly why it's going to do *your people* good. This will come out. Or do you think we're the only ones who know? Please. Now tell me: Do you want to be the sort who's going to pretend this isn't happening or the sort who's going to start something new?"

All three remained silent. Pel felt as if their bodies were levitating, but only from the knees up.

"Thank you for trusting me," the spy said. "I really appreciate it, though maybe you just think I'm an idiot. Regardless, thank you. You've put the fate of our misfortune in my hands."

He laughed quietly, then turned around again and walked away.

"I know," said Cradoq, "it's irresponsible to trust the enemy, but I think if he's actually convinced, he'll be a much more effective ally than if we trick him. What do you think?"

"He might betray us, but it doesn't matter," Pel said, as she recalled what she'd seen right before the spy arrived: his emotional pupil. "What matters is that *now he knows*. Now he's inoculated."

Cradoq moved his hand gently, as if swinging a ladybug from his fingers, which emitted a curtain of smoke that looked like a small misty dawn.

APPENDIX 15, NUMBER 2:
THE EXPLORATION OF AGENT PROBII

When this planet—the ninth to which the iotafication machines had sent survivors millennia ago—was discovered, the first thing we did was confirm that its inhabitants were human. Aside from a few small mutations, such as the growth of the pinna and an elongation of the fingers, it was determined that they had indeed remained perfectly human. The second thing was to decipher the language in which they communicated, a feat that proved far more difficult than anticipated, not because decoding it seemed impossible, or because they spoke more than one language (a perfectly human possibility), but because what we found defied the very notion of "language."

The discovery was made by Agent Probii, one of our best, who despite having undertaken extraordinary research was incapable of drawing the logical conclusions that would have saved his life. This report is based on the data he collected.

Agent Probii's first days undercover were particularly disconcerting, because the city (if it can be so called) in which he arrived was lacking in stable landmarks: where one day there was a paved corner, that night he found a wasteland; where one night there had been a streetlight, the following morning he found only a box of cats. Eventually he understood that actually this urban fugacity (if indeed we can employ this adjective or that noun) was providing the precise information he was looking for.

It is not that the local language is unstable but that there are multiple languages, and each individual speaks only their own. Alone, at home, cooking, out for a walk, but never in dialogue. The differences between how each inhabitant speaks extend far beyond the lexical. For instance, to say "I'm alive," one can employ multiple adjectives: to be stressed, alert, flowing, tremulous; but there are clear syntactical differences, like so:

Stressedme.

I-alert, i-alert.

Meflowing postflow.

Sirtremulouso.

Though not every language studied possesses agreement in gender and number (the planet's inhabitants, it would seem, are not particularly interested in enumerating objects, and though some languages recognize two genders, others identify up to fourteen), one common characteristic is agreement of spirit. A complete sentence may employ prefixes, infixes, or suffixes to denote the spirit in which the action is performed.

Thus, the aforementioned examples might become:

Distressedme.

Inpeace-alert, i-alert.

Melliflowous postflow.

Sirtremulousobad.

And so forth.

This uproarious concerto of voices, which appear not to respond to one another, wrote Probii, in fact slowly spawn a series of intelligible utterances, asserting the desires and opinions of each speaker, although these are expressed not via a single tongue, as it were, but in a language that, while it includes words, does not depend upon them.

In order to understand it, Probii began to observe people at various phases of development. He established that while babies seem to share the same tongue in early stages of verbalization, over the course of their development it is forgotten or stops making sense. Thus begins a period of introspection that lasts until the onset of puberty, when, after an endless silence, adolescents see how their bodies change and quickly learn the gradations, accents, and ellipses of their physiognomy; they perfect the figuration of their flesh until arriving at what is the planet's lingua franca: copulation.

Thereafter the planet's inhabitants copulate in every way and with every participant needed in order to express themselves with precision. What is being expressed by placing one hand in one place and the other in another varies quite a bit depending on what the mouth is doing, how many others are participating, and how slowly it is being done. The nose is vital in the communication of nuance. When words emerge during the act, they are spaced out—not pragmatic objects but the accent on a sentence already being spoken with hips or teeth.

In this way relations are entered into, parties organized, secrets revealed, recipes passed down, detailed instructions given. The planning of the city's biggest bridge, for instance, required the amatory efforts of ninety-seven people at once.

Clearly it was the prospect of learning such sexual sophistication that led Agent Probii to his perdition. As per the last report filed, Probii singled out one person with whom to enter into contact, but, as he was incapable of understanding the multiple signs exchanged before reaching that level of communication, what he did was study the language of the person in question, learn the nuts and bolts, and come up with a sentence that, in his judgment, would suffice for the purposes of proceeding to copulation. The sentence, in the most pragmatic of terms, was akin to "Me too please."

The precise meaning, however, is not important in the least. It may be that the person in question wasn't even paying attention to what Probii said. The most likely scenario, as per our subsequent reconstructions via prudent investigations involving minimal interference, is that the very act of suddenly turning up and attempting to usurp the person's most intimate of possessions—*their* unique and inimitable tongue—was interpreted as a heinous act. Whether this exposed him as a spy or a devil is of no concern; the response was the same: Agent Probii's throat was summarily slit no sooner than he'd demonstrated his linguistic prowess.

It seems likely that in the relatively near future they will be the ones to establish contact with us. If we've correctly interpreted the massive orgy that has been taking place at the planet's equator for some two years now, they're in the process of imagining a spaceship.

LIVING MUSCLE

There is a very distant star, nestled in a dense spiral galaxy, that looks to be approaching adolescence; classified by a couple numbers and a couple letters no less significant than any other possible numbers and letters. It is orbited by several planets outside the habitable zone: frostily hostile or belligerently incandescent and misty. Except for one halfway along, whose orbit places it, at a certain time of year, nearly as close to the star as the hotheads, and at another nearly as far as the frosties.

At first sight it's a compact planet, no volcanoes or fault lines, but it extends and distends at regular intervals, and is permanently enveloped in thunderstorms.

It's a planet made of living muscle.

When approaching the sun it contracts and relaxes while rotating on its axis to keep from cooking in the star's heat. When it is distant, it retracts, as if searching for a warm nucleus within so as not to turn into a diamond.

We've sent a considerable number of probes to discover what lies beneath the soft tissue, but as soon as they disturb the surface, it begins to vibrate steadily until they are brought down.

One thing we have managed to discover is that on its trajectory from the coldest to the warmest part of the solar system, the planet emits a sequence of vibrations following the pattern do-si, re-si, mi-si, fa-si, sol-si, and then si-sol, si-fa, si-mi, si-re, si-do, over the millions and millions of iotas it travels. It's less an inexpressive sequence than a perfectly *human* humming, some say. And occasionally it completes an entire orbit in silence.

We have decided to send no more probes.

Nor have we assigned it a name.

THE LAST ONES

Before becoming the first human to cross the Atlantic on foot, he was the first to see a snail crawl along the stalk of a plant. He watched it while about to begin his voyage. That wasn't the worst of Reu's voyages—the ship and the plank had been lonelier, and the rock had been scarier—but none took longer than the crossing of every last iota of the Atlantic on foot.

He hadn't planned on doing so, it was just that the sea had devoured the earth and the trash had devoured the sea, so he commenced walking till he reached the end of dry land and then kept on walking across the solid crust and by the end of the day he could no longer see the ruins behind him—the humongous ruins of the United States embassy, the angular ruins of the Chinese embassy, the monumental ruins of the Nicaraguan embassy— and that was when he decided there was no turning back.

He walked for two years across the putrid surface of the solid crust: he learned how not to die by gnawing on it and how not to dissolve in its salt at night; he healed his own bones when the wind whipped him through the air like a rag and flung him onto the stiff waves.

He was perpetually dazzled by the glare, but every once in a while he glimpsed shadows beneath the crust, brooding their bodies from one side to another and bashing themselves against the surface.

Once he caught sight of an old man, inexplicably gleeful, jigging from one little plastic islet to the next. They waved at each other, arms aloft; he managed to make out the other man's silhouette, stretched tall against the glare of the crust, and at that precise moment an enormous, jagged mouth rose up around the old man's feet and carried him down to the depths of that filthy chowder.

He met one of those monsters himself after chancing upon the last human beings he'd come across before reaching the far side of the ocean. A small colony of the lost, who'd ended up banding together as the currents thrust them toward the vortex in which they now dwelled. They spent their miserable waking hours patching cracks in the scab, but they'd learned to fish for those tiny-eyed beasts whose maws took up half their bodies. They used their hard, sinewy flesh for food, their stiff whiskers to sew, and their fangs to make spears.

They told Reu he could stay with them and they were willing to share, but theirs was a will with no bone to it—he knew his kind. The time would come when they were shoving one another out of the way to keep from being bit. Even if they offered company, it was still human company, which is good only for short spells.

He arrived in time to slip onto the last ship. Its destination was a rock nearing the outer edge of the solar system. If they managed to land on it, they'd be taken who knew where, but that was the least of it.

Either some visionary or someone truly terrified had come up with the idea of overhauling asteroids for space travel. It had taken generations, but once it had been imagined, they inevitably ended up pulling it off. It was claimed they'd built stations from which spaceships set off in search of another rock: it was said that at those stations there were ships—much larger, much faster ships—that could take them to a hospitable place; there was talk of planets on which one could almost live well, and even of rocks on which plants and animals lived.

He persuaded the last of the stevedores—last one to last one—to let him hide in the cargo hold. He had no window from which to watch the scum of chemical elements in which he'd begun his time in the universe shrinking away. He knew they'd abandoned Earth when boxes began to bob a few iotas up into the iotas of available space, as though celebrating.

Then cold and near asphyxiation, until they hauled him from the hold and hurled him into a cavern in the rock. Though the cavern was packed, the danger lay not in being crushed to death, no: People agonized in an exceedingly slow battle to get close to the ducts spewing food and oxygen. The rock's inhabitants strangled one another feebly, scratching flesh with more hatred than force; they pulled one another's hair and slowly broke one another's bones. Then, with sickening efficiency, the detritus was pushed toward a hatch, where it was sucked up and sent out into space.

They floated in that mist of bodies for what on Earth might have been weeks, and finally they reached the station. *It really did exist.*

It was a platform topped with a dome. And it was pressurized, but a glass panel running from the floor to the ceiling separated new arrivals from those already there. Reu surveyed the space from his side, a rectangle of darkness illuminated every so often by enormous ships (*they really did exist*) taking off from the dome's ring.

The side where the first ones waited slowly emptied, as the last ones watched ships take off one after another, until they were the only ones left. Before departing, the first ones lined up on their side a series of small plank-ships on which only one person could fit, lying down and facing front. One of them approached the glass and explained how they worked: the planks pulsated; between one interval and the next, each occupant would be in suspended animation; they had enough energy for the initial thrust that would launch them from the deck, plus a bit more that could be used to change direction, so better use it wisely.

"With a little luck, someone will find you out there," he said, forcing himself to act like he believed his own words. "It has been known to happen."

He opened the hatch separating the two sides of the dome and before the last ones had time to take note of their newly acquired solitude, he climbed into his ship and took off.

There were no fights over who got the plank-ships, for the majority decided to stay put. This couldn't be the end, they thought. That was what he thought too, but he opted to think it while embarking on his firefly voyage.

One single shifting light in the abyss. So slowly did it shift that he was unsure what it was until he saw it approach his plank-ship. A metal-covered cetacean, black, crude, with a bubble of light in its belly.

As he got closer, Reu saw that inside the bubble was a person, *pedaling*.

He used what fuel he had left to turn his plank toward the cetacean, but there wasn't enough. It was going to pass him by. Then the cetacean changed direction, positioned itself in front of his plank, and opened a hatch that swallowed him up.

As soon as he'd unstiffened, Reu exited the plank-ship and began walking down rusty-smelling corridors and up creaky stairwells. He found the bubble at the back of the ship and for a moment could discern nothing, so blinding was its light, but finally he was able to see that the pedaler was a woman. Her body was slightly tensed with the mechanical movement but her face indicated no effort at all; she stared at an instrument panel before her. When finally she looked at Reu, she did so as though he provoked no curiosity.

"Anyone else with you?" she asked.

Reu shook his head. She turned back to the instrument panel.

"Not good," she went on. "That means I'll have to eat you."

She pedaled some more. Then turned to look at him and smiled.

"After we finish off all the food," she added. "I've got plenty."

It had been so long since anyone had made a joke that for a moment he thought she was insane. Then, almost as a vestigial reflex, he too smiled.

Her name was Pel. She explained that pedaling was the only way to amass energy. She'd used some of it to alter her position in the infinite quadrant a few iotas in order to reach him, so now they'd have to work to replace it.

Pel asked him where he was hoping to go.

"I just want to keep moving."

Pel nodded and her pupils dilated as though she was going to say something terrible. But instead what she said had a different precision:

"You don't smell like metal."

She got off the stationary bike, put her nose to Reu's neck, and slid her hand behind his head. And then she reconned the bony peaks of his spine and he slipped his hands under her sweaty

T-shirt; and they attested and attested and attested and attested to the fact they were still made of water, and that flesh was still holding its own in the universe.

The last memory he had of anything like *that* from Earth was one of that afternoon in the gullet of an embassy in ruins. He'd taken refuge there shortly before he began his walk across the Atlantic and had discovered that a microclimate spiked with trees had been preserved. Discovered it as if it had just rolled out before him, but in reality nothing was moving, everything was still and silent, though it wasn't a dead stillness: he could feel the afternoon *taking place*. Not things slipping by but the time in between the things. Then he saw something else moving, a snail making its way along a stalk as if the world's collapse was of no concern to it at all.

That was how it felt in the space the ship traversed as he and Pel relived the beast with two backs. What planet could possibly beat that one? What need was there to beat it?

But a few million iotas later she said:

"We're almost there."

Reu was pedaling at the time and stopped to turn and look at her, uncomprehending.

"The station," Pel went on. "There's another one."

She paused and continued.

"But bodies depart from this one."

The first ones knew of the existence of hospitable planets, but they were too distant to be reachable by ship, so they devised a way to deotafy the body and then send it, iota by iota, until the machine found a world where it could be reotafied: for an immeasurable time, which the body conceived only as a jolt of quasars. Pel wasn't sure how many people had managed to travel this way, only that after one or two generations the system collapsed and the deotafication stations rusted over or floated off into space and disappeared.

But she knew where one was.

Soon they sighted the station, and as Pel steered the cetacean toward it, Reu began to wonder whether he really wanted to be with other humans again.

Pel didn't wonder.

"We're going to make it," she said.

It was a fragile and beautiful plural.

Rather than a dome, this platform had an exceedingly long chimney, far longer than a hundred times the length of the cetacean. They docked. They put on their suits and entered.

There were two rows of cabins facing each other and a control panel at the back. Pel confirmed that she knew how it worked and began testing it while he inspected the cabins to check for any obvious defects.

Suddenly he felt the energy source kick in and the platform began to rattle; the chimney pressurized, its ancient materials active once more, creaky but alert. Pel kept operating the controls and two cabins lit up, one on each side, and began in sync to change shape, like a second hand, with each second corresponding to a different-shaped human.

"It has to be now," Pel said, heading for one of the cabins.

Reu faltered.

"What if we end up on opposite ends of the universe?"

Pel looked at him like he'd said something absurd. She turned and entered her cabin. Before the door closed she said something he couldn't hear, though he saw her lips move.

Reu entered his cabin and from within watched as Pel's cabin shaped itself more precisely to her body with every second. Just before it molded to her body like a black peapod, Reu realized that Pel had said:

"We're always on opposite ends of the universe."

He thought she'd said it as if she were talking about something that could be remedied, the way overturning a cup on the tablecloth would have been, in another age.

And every little iota in his body began covering the endless iotas along the way.

WARNING

If you would like to skip to the end of this Authorization, designating all terms and conditions as read, click HERE.

None of the uses promoted in commercials for the product you have just purchased or the packaging in which you received it should be viewed as guaranteed or recommended, as such uses are demonstrated solely as purely hypothetical and not legally binding in any way. Should you wish to proceed now to the end of this Authorization designating all terms and conditions read, click HERE.

The Rand Corporation is not responsible for any physical or psychological consequences that might result from the use of the product in any of the following hypothetical ways: as a transmission device, conjuring tool, paperweight, cooking utensil, object of worship, birth control, decoration. If you would like to skip to the end of this Authorization and designate all terms and conditions as having been read, click HERE.

Furthermore, acceptance of the terms and conditions set forth in this Authorization (if you would like to give your Authorization now, click HERE) likewise entails legal cession of the following rights to the Rand Corporation (including its affiliates: the Kalashnikov Corporation, the High-Smith Corporation,

Vgany Meat Company, Genesis Corporation, IPAM Business School, and Athenaeum Paper Mill, as well as any of the various corporations and their respective affiliates that might join the Rand Corporation at some point in the future): the right to use personal photographs, the right to use the Customer Service Department, the right to use affectionate names for pets who may have been made aware of the Rand Corporation via the product, assuming without admitting that the product may be able to transmit such information (excluded from these names are "Baby" and "Champ," currently under legal dispute between the Rand Corporation and Nica Corporation), the right to inquire, the right to reply. Further, the buyer renounces their right to file any claims regarding any idea deemed by the Rand Corporation to be a NewIdea™. If you would now like to skip to the end of this Authorization designating its terms as read, click HERE.

With this Authorization you consent to have any information about your use of the product utilized in but not limited to electoral campaigns, national security, meat product recycling, pharmaceutical experimentation, cosmetics research, psychological warfare, market studies, and collected prose.

For more details on the rights you are ceding, send a request in writing in a sealed envelope to the offices of the Rand Corporation, whose address you may or may not find in small print at the end of this Authorization, although nothing guarantees a review of your request in the upcoming fiscal period.

To give your Authorization, click HERE.

TRANSLATOR'S NOTE

Despite growing up a voracious reader, I was never a sci-fi fan. But then, in college, I took an African American literature course in which we read Octavia E. Butler's *Imago* and that all changed (shout-out to Professor Frances Smith Foster). Until that time, I had stereotyped science fiction as a genre for the maladapted Dungeons & Dragons crowd. Sadly, it had not dawned on me, ever the literalist, that positing alternate worlds—whether utopic or dystopic or other—was in itself a commentary on our world. On its injustices, inequities, and absurdities. That it was all metaphor, or at least could be read as such. It was the science part of science fiction that had left me cold. Imagining new possibilities, defying what we take to be true, that was something I could get behind. And that is something Yuri Herrera's writing always does.

It would be redundant to say that *Ten Planets* is something of a departure from Yuri's previous work. His writing is nothing if not experimental and everything he writes is something of a departure. But in it, certain preoccupations and predilections are revisited: the power of language; the relationship between art and hegemony; the pushing of borders, be they geographical (interplanetary), temporal, generic (is this "really" sci-fi? who cares?), or lexical.

One lexical issue has to do with standard versus non-standard usage. Yuri has spoken in the past about selecting particular words he consciously wants to use (or avoid) in a given work. I did not ask him whether he'd done this in *Ten Planets*, but it struck me that one of the words he'd decided to use was *ápice*, often translated as *shred, speck, ounce, inch, bit,* or *iota*. For instance, in common parlance you might say someone does not give one *ápice* about your opinion, or that a person has not an *ápice* of sense. But Yuri, unsurprisingly, very rarely uses *ápice* in standard ways. Instead, his characters are separated by *ápices,* or sail through *ápices,* or turn into *ápices.* They are literalized, embodied, materialized, demetaphorized.

Words are frequently polysemous, which is to say a single term may have multiple meanings. For example, in addition to the definitions listed above, *ápice* can also mean both *tip* (of your tongue, say) and *apex* (as in geometry: is that a science?). So the same word used several times in Spanish might be rendered many different ways in English, whether due to polysemy or to the tone, shading, or connotation it carries in a given context. Some translators are more concerned by this, striving for a one-to-one translation whenever possible, and some are less so. I'm on the lesser end of the spectrum. It troubles me, but just ~~a bit~~ an iota. Barring a concrete reason why A needs to be translated as B in every instance, I will use a range of English words for a single word in Spanish. And yet, I have chosen to translate *ápice* as *iota* in English throughout *Ten Planets*. Every ~~inch~~ iota of my being felt compelled not to stray from this lexical choice every time an *ápice* cropped up. In part because it is used in idiosyncratic ways in the Spanish. In part because aside from meaning "a tiny amount" (and being the etymological root of "jot"), it has, to my ear, a more science-y ring than the other options and as such lends truthiness. But what is more, it refers explicitly to the ninth star in a constellation. It's a space-y word. Stellar in all respects.

Another linguistic issue, this one more routine in terms of translation, has to do with syntax. The first sentence of the first story ("The Science of Extinction") reads: "When the man realized he'd soon be lost, he took out a small yellow card, wrote four words, and placed it on the sill of the window he looked out every day upon waking." On first glance, it contains no obvious challenges. There is no neologism, no punning, no cultural or historical reference to matters that would be clearly understood by a Spanish readership but not an English one. Still, there were probably eight or ten versions of this sentence that I considered. Earlier drafts began with a gerund ("On realizing . . ."). This syntax enabled me to delay using a subject ("When *the man* realized") but also raised the register, giving the very first words of the book too formal a tone—and making the use of "on waking" at the end of the sentence problematic. Initially, too, my inclination was for the man to place the yellow card on the *windowsill* and rather than the *sill of the window*. But the modifying phrase *he looked out every day* that immediately follows then became illogical, since of course the man is not looking out the sill itself.

There were a number of minor considerations as well. Should he *write* four words or write them *down*? Should he *wake up* rather than wake? Would it be better to simply *take* the card rather than take it *out*? Phrasal verbs: a common issue in translation and the bane of many English-language learners. Sometimes, as in the case of this opening sentence, phrasal verbs serve to nuance the tone, formality, or rhythm of a statement. Ultimately, my sense of the rhythm played a role in determining when to use them.

The biggest problem, however, had to do with the subject. The Spanish sentence* contains not a single subject pronoun or noun. Not one *he*. Nary a *man*. English, tragically, does not allow us to dispense with subjects: *When realized soon would be lost, took out a yellow card* might make a point and even function in syntactically experimental prose, but that's not what's going on here. So, how to avoid using "he" five or six times in a single sentence—which would create clunky-sounding repetition not present in the Spanish—while also avoiding a stilted start? My answer to this question was to once use *the man*, once insert a gerund, and aim for the other uses of *he* to be rhythmically unstressed (what I mean by this is that, were you to read it aloud, you would likely stress the italicized words: When the *man* realized he'd *soon* be *lost*, he *took* out a small yellow card, *wrote* four words, and *placed* it on the *sill* of the window he *looked* out every day upon *waking*).

A love and respect for language is evident in everything Yuri writes, and language itself is regularly a theme. He constantly pushes linguistic borders. He neologizes, he rescues archaic words, he recovers words and expressions in disuse, he verbs nouns. He finds lexical ways to inject energy, life, surprise, and humor. In "The Objects" (the first one, since two stories bear exactly the same title: and why not?), for instance, protagonist Velia wakes to realize that her daughter is not home and attempts to track her using something resembling GPS, on something that resembles a smartphone. In Spanish, the device is called a *Tenmeaquí* (literally: *keepmehere*). Initially, I called it a *Hereyougo*. The device deter-

---

* Cuando comprendió que pronto estaría perdido tomó una pequeña tarjeta amarilla, apuntó cuatro palabras y la colocó en el quicio de la ventana por la que todos los días se asomaba al despertar.

mines her actions, sending her warnings and notifications, telling her to turn this way, slow down, take a detour, and so on.

When I asked Yuri about the name, he told me he'd named the "idiotizing device" after an expression mothers used to use with children to keep them out of the way, under control, occupied. They would say things like: Go tell nana to make you some *tenmeaquí* tea. The internet offered several slight variations (Tell the neighbor to give you a kilo of *tenmeaquí*, Go ask your auntie for a bouquet of *tenmeaquí*). *Hereyougo* seemed to function in a denotative sense, i.e., it sounded plausible as a device that might guide you, determine your route. And it was polysemous, offering the additional sense of *voilà*. But it lacked irony, didn't suggest an object inducing passivity or mindlessness; a *Hereyougo* is not an apparatus that keeps the populace from thinking. Plus I wanted a word with more of a ring to it, ideally a portmanteau.

Brainstorming and translator forums led to other options. *Dummy* was the first of these. Americans aren't familiar with this term as it's used in the UK (i.e., as what we call a *pacifier*), and it struck me as apt. A device that keeps you quiet and also means stupid. *Spellphone* was in the running for a very long time, but in the end, I felt it would be too easy to think only *how do you spell . . . ?* and not of *casting a spell*. *Ensorcellphone* is a fabulous portmanteau, but I didn't even know the verb *ensorcell* (to enchant) prior to diving into this quandary. Finally, I came up with Miniminder, which to my mini-mind suggests multiple readings. It could be a stand-in for oneself, a mini-me. It could be a small mind. And it could be a diminutive minder, i.e., babysitter or thing that looks after someone. What I sought was less a word that literally referred to something mothers might tell children when they wanted to get them out of their hair than a term that was playful, sonorous, and polysemous. The English translation could not *be* the same as *Tenmeaquí*, but it could *do* something quite similar. This, of course, was my interpretation and if you asked ten different translators, they would come up with ten different solutions. One for each planet.

There's something both daunting and cringe-making about the idea of writing an afterword for a book written by a living author who is fluent in English, regularly gives interviews, and speaks eloquently about his own work. And yet here I am. My intention, however, is not to elucidate for readers the underlying significance of *Ten Planets*. There is no univocal reading, no terrestrial secret code to unlock. Moreover, one constant in both Yuri's writing and his generous perspective is the belief that meaning is never fixed, and readers will make their own interpretations, as did I. His work, like so many of its words, is polysemous. So my hope is instead to illuminate one iota, *un ápice*, of translation in general, and of the planets contained in this book in particular.

Lisa Dillman
Decatur, Georgia
May 2022

YURI HERRERA was born in Actopan, México, in 1970 and is the author of the novels *Kingdom Cons, Signs Preceding the End of the World,* and *The Transmigration of Bodies,* which have been translated into many languages. In 2016 he shared with translator Lisa Dillman the Best Translated Book Award for *Signs Preceding the End of the World.* That same year, he published *Talud,* a collection of short stories, and received the Anna Seghers Prize at the Academy of Arts, Berlin. His latest book is *A Silent Fury: The El Bordo Mine Fire.* He is a professor of creative writing and literature at Tulane University in New Orleans.

LISA DILLMAN is a translator from Los Angeles and lives in Atlanta. She has translated more than thirty novels, including all of Yuri Herrera's books available in English. Other writers she has translated include Pilar Quintana, Alejandra Costamagna, and Graciela Mochkovsky. In 2020 her translation of Quintana's *The Bitch* was a finalist for the National Book Award in Translated Literature. She teaches in the Department of Spanish and Portuguese at Emory University.

The text of *Ten Planets* is set in Crimson Text.
Book design by Rachel Holscher.
Composition by Bookmobile Design & Digital
Publisher Services, Minneapolis, Minnesota.
Manufactured by McNaughton & Gunn on acid-free,
100 percent postconsumer wastepaper.